KRISTI'S BLOG—Day 1

Lorikeet Island: surrounded by the bluest ocean on the planet, perfect weather. I've lasted the first hour without making any major gaffs in front of the cameras. Then again, have sat petrified, watching Jared act all manly by scoping out the lay of the land.

Don't know why he's bothering. Not like we'll get attacked by any wild animals, right?

Yikes! What was that growling sound?

Oh, only my stomach. Woman does not survive on soda and fresh air alone. Time to rustle up lunch. Baked beans on campfire toast?

I miss Sydney already.

JARED'S BLOG—Day 1

Not a bad spot. Might take up fishing. Kristi brought too many shoes. She's such a girl.

Do you like stories that are fun and flirty?

Then you'll ♥ Harlequin® Romance's new miniseries—
where love and laughter are guaranteed!

If you love romantic comedies, look for

The Fun Factor

Warm and witty stories of falling in love

**Look out for more Fun Factor stories
coming soon!**

NICOLA MARSH

Deserted Island, Dreamy Ex!

The Fun Factor

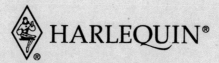

HARLEQUIN®

TORONTO • NEW YORK • LONDON
AMSTERDAM • PARIS • SYDNEY • HAMBURG
STOCKHOLM • ATHENS • TOKYO • MILAN • MADRID
PRAGUE • WARSAW • BUDAPEST • AUCKLAND

Recycling programs
for this product may
not exist in your area.

ISBN-13: 978-0-373-74053-6

DESERTED ISLAND, DREAMY EX!

First North American Publication 2010.

Copyright © 2010 by Nicola Marsh.

Nicola Marsh has always had a passion for writing and reading. As a youngster she devoured books when she should have been sleeping, and later kept a diary whose content could be an epic in itself! These days, when she's not enjoying life with her husband and son in her home city of Melbourne, she's at her computer, creating the romances she loves in her dream job. Visit Nicola's Web site at www.nicolamarsh.com for the latest news of her books.

This one's for all my newfound friends on Twitter.
Tweeting with you is a blast!

CHAPTER ONE

Stranded *Survival Tip #1*
Your past is only a line call away.

KRISTI WILDE picked up the single blush-pink
rose, twirled it under her nose, closed her eyes and
inhaled the subtle fragrance.

She should call Lars and thank him but… Her
eyes snapped open, landed on the trite card he'd
probably sent to countless other women, and she
promptly tossed the store-bought, cellophane-
wrapped rose in the bin.

The only reason she'd agreed to a date with
Sydney's top male model was to gain a firsthand
look at a rival promotions company's much
touted coup in landing the Annabel Modelling
Agency as a client.

The fact Lars was six four, ripped, tanned and
gorgeous had merely been added incentive.

Walking into Guillaume hand in hand with a

guy like Lars had been an ego trip. But that was about as exciting as things got for the night.

Lars had the looks but his personality could put a bunch of hyperactive kids to sleep. While she'd scoped out the opposition, feasted on fabulous French food and swilled pricey champagne, Lars had droned on about himself…and on…and on.

She'd faked interest, been the epitome of a dewy-eyed, suitably impressed bimbo hanging on his every word. She'd do anything for a promotion these days. Excluding the horizontal catwalk, which was exactly what Lars had had in mind the moment they'd stepped into the elevator at the end of the night.

The rose might be an apology. Then again, considering his smug assuredness she'd succumb to his charms next time, he was probably hedging his bets.

Wrinkling her nose, she nudged the bin away with her Christian Louboutin fuchsia patent peep-toes and darted a glance at her online calendar.

Great, just enough time to grab a soy chai latte before heading to the Sydney Cricket Ground for a football promotion.

She grabbed her bag, opened the door, in time for her boss to sweep into the room on four-inch Choos, a swathe of crushed ebony velvet bellowing around her like a witch's cloak, a cloud of Chanel No 5 in her wake.

'Hey, Ros, I was just on my way out—'

'You're not going anywhere.'

Rosanna waved a wad of paper under her nose and pointed at her desk.

'Sit. Listen.'

Kristi rolled her eyes. 'The bossy routine doesn't impress me so much any more after watching you dance the tango with that half-naked waiter at the Christmas party last year. And after that romp through the chocolate fountain at the PR awards night. And that incident with the stripper at Shay's hen night—'

'Zip it.'

Despite her being a driven professional business-woman, Rosanna's pride in her wild side endeared her to co-workers. Kristi couldn't imagine speaking to any other boss the way she did to Ros.

'Take a look at this.'

Rosanna's kohled eyes sparkled with mischief as she handed her the sheaf of documents, clapping her hands once she'd delivered her bundle.

Kristi hadn't seen her boss this excited since Endorse This had snatched a huge client out from under a competitor's nose.

'You're going to thank me.'

Rosanna started pacing, shaking her hands out, muttering under her breath in the exact way she did while brainstorming with her PR team.

Curious as to what had her boss this hyped, Kristi scanned the top document, her confusion increasing rather than diminishing.

'What's this reality show documentary about?'

It sounded interesting, if you were crazy enough to want to be stranded on an island with a stranger for a week. 'We doing the PR for it?'

Rosanna shook her head, magenta-streaked corkscrew curls flying.

'No. One better.'

Flipping pages, Kristi spied an entry form.

'You thinking of entering?'

Rosanna grinned, the evil grin of a lioness about to pounce on a defenceless gazelle.

'Not me.'

'Then what…?'

Realisation dawned as Rosanna's grin widened.

'Oh, no, you haven't?'

Rosanna perched on the edge of her desk, studying her mulberry manicured talons at length.

'I entered your details for the female applicant.' She gestured to the flyer, pointed at the fine print. 'You've been chosen. Just you and some hot stud on a deserted island for seven days and seven long, hot, glorious nights. Cool, huh?'

There were plenty of words to describe what her boss had done.

Cool wasn't one of them.

Kristi dropped the entry form as if it were radio-active waste, tentatively poked it with her toe, before inhaling deep, calming breaths. Rosanna might be tolerant but there was no point getting wound up to the point she could happily strangle her boss.

'I want you to turn Survivor for a week.'

This had to be a joke, one of Rosanna's bizarre tests she spontaneously sprang on employees at random to test their company loyalty.

Clenching her fist so hard the documents crinkled, she placed them on the desk, desperately trying to subdue the buzzing in her head to form a coherent argument to convince her boss there wasn't a chance she'd do this.

Only one way Rosanna would listen to reason: appeal to her business side.

'Sound's interesting, but I'm snowed under with jobs at the moment. I can't just up and leave for a week.'

Rosanna sprang off her desk as if she hadn't spoken, snapped her fingers.

'You know Elliott J. Barnaby, the hottest producer in town?'

Kristi nodded warily as Rosanna picked up a flyer, waved it under her nose. 'He's making a documentary, based on the reality-show phenomenon sweeping the world. Two people, placed on an island, with limited resources, for a week.'

'Sounds like a blast.'

Rosanna ignored her sarcasm. 'Prize money is a hundred grand.'

'What?'

Kristi tried to read over Rosanna's shoulder. 'You never told me that part.'

'Didn't I? Perhaps I didn't get around to mentioning it, what with your overwhelming excitement and all.'

Kristi stuck out her tongue as she speed-read the prize details.

A hundred big ones. A heck of a lot of money. And if she was crazy enough to go along with her boss's ludicrous scheme, she knew exactly what she'd do with it.

For an instant, the memory of dinner with her sister Meg last night flashed into her head.

Meg's shabby, cubbyhole apartment in outer Sydney, the sounds of ear-splitting verbal abuse from the quarrelling couple next door interspersed with the ranting of rival street gangs outside her window. The threadbare furniture, the stack of unpaid bills on the kitchen counter, the lack of groceries in the fridge.

And Prue, her adorable seven-year-old niece, the only person who managed to draw a smile from her weary mum these days.

After what she'd been through, Meg was doing

it tough yet wouldn't accept a cent. What if the money wasn't part of her savings that Meg refused to touch? Would that make a difference to her sister's pride?

'Healthy prize, huh?'

Kristi didn't like the maniacal gleam in Rosanna's astute gaze. She'd seen that look before. Ros lived for Endorse This; the company wasn't Sydney's best PR firm for nothing. While a fun and fair boss, she was a corporate dynamo who expected nothing short of brilliance from her employees.

And every time she got that gleam, it meant a new client was up for grabs, someone whose promotion would add another feather to Endorse This's ever-expanding cap.

Deliberately trying to blot out the memory of Meg's apartment and the unnatural hollows in her niece's cheeks, Kristi handed the flyer back.

'Sure, the money's impressive, but not worth shacking up with some stranger for a week, and having the whole disastrous experience filmed.'

Rosanna's injected lips thinned, her determined stare brooking no argument.

'You're doing this.'

Kristi's mouth dropped open and her boss promptly placed a finger under her chin and shut it for her.

'I had a call from Channel Nine last week. They're checking out PR firms for a new island reality show, Survivor with a twist, they said. That's why I entered you. If you do this, we're set!'

Oh, no. No, no, no!

If the gleam in Rosanna's eyes had raised her hackles, it had nothing on the sickly sweet smile reminiscent of a witch offering Hansel and Gretel a huge chunk of gingerbread.

'And, of course, you'll be in charge of that whole account.'

'That's not fair,' she blurted, wishing she'd kept her mouth shut when Rosanna's smile waned.

'Which part? The part where you help Endorse This score the biggest client this year? Or the part where you're virtually assured a promotion because of it? Discounting the chance to win a hundred grand, of course.'

Kristi shot Rosanna a death glare that had little effect, Ros's smugness adding to the churning in the pit of her stomach.

She had no choice.

She had to do this.

If the promotion wasn't incentive enough, the chance to win a hundred grand was. Meg deserved better, much better. Her sweet, naïve, resilient sister deserved to have all her dreams come true after what she'd been through.

Forcing an enthusiastic smile that must've appeared half grimace, she shrugged.

'Fine, I'll do it.'

'Great. You've got a meeting with the producer in a few hours. Fill me in on the details later.'

Rosanna thrust the flyer into her hands, glanced at her watch. 'I'll get back to Channel Nine, let them know the latest.'

As Rosanna strutted towards the door Kristi knew she'd made the right decision, despite being shanghaied into it.

She'd worked her butt off the last six months, desperate for a promotion, and landing Channel Nine as a client would shoot her career to the stars.

As for the prize money, she'd do whatever it took to win it. No way would she accept anything less than Meg using every last brass razoo of it.

The promotion and the prize money; sane, logical reasons to go through with this. But a week on an island with a stranger? Could it be any worse?

As she rifled through the paperwork, Rosanna paused at the door, raised a finger.

'Did I mention you'll be stranded on the island with Jared Malone?'

CHAPTER TWO

Stranded *Survival Tip #2*
Be sure to schedule your mini-meltdown for off-camera.

JARED strode into North Bondi's Icebergs and headed for Elliott's usual table, front and centre to the glass overlooking Sydney's most famous beach.

His mango smoothie was waiting alongside Elliott's double-shot espresso, his mate nothing if not predictable.

When he neared the table, Elliott glanced up from a stack of paperwork, folded his iron-rimmed glasses, placed them next to his coffee and glanced at his watch.

'Glad you could eventually make it.'

Jared shrugged, pointed at his gammy knee. 'Rehab session went longer than anticipated.'

Elliott's eyes narrowed. 'Hot physio?'

'Hot cruciate ligament, more like it.'

The familiar pinch of pain grabbed as he sat. 'The

cruciate healed well after the reconstruction but the ongoing inflammation has the medicos baffled.'

Elliott frowned. 'You're seeing the best, right?'

Jared rolled his eyes. 'Yes, Mum.'

'Putz.'

'The putz that's going to win you another of those film gongs you covet so much.'

Jared jerked a thumb at the pile of documents in front of him.

'Let me guess. The usual disclaimers that anything I say or do on TV, you won't be held responsible.'

'Something like that.'

Elliott pulled the top document, slid it across the table towards him.

'Here's the gist of it.'

Jared barely glanced at the fine print, having already heard Elliott extol the virtues of his documentary at length.

Stranded on an island with a stranger for a week was the last thing he felt like doing, but if it convinced Sydney's disadvantaged kids the Activate recreation centre was the place for them, he'd do it.

He'd spent the bulk of his life in the spotlight, his career and private life under scrutiny, providing fodder for the paparazzi. He'd hated it. Time to put all that intrusion to good use, starting with a week's worth of free publicity money couldn't buy.

Elliott's award-winning documentaries were watched by millions, his cutting-edge work discussed by everyone; around water coolers, at the school gates, on the streets, everyone talked about Elliott's topical stuff.

With a prime-time viewing slot, free advertisements would cost mega bucks so when Elliot had proposed his deal, he'd jumped at it. He'd much rather spend a billion on the centre and equipment than publicity.

Millions would see the centre on national TV, hear about what it offered, and hopefully spread the word. That was what he was counting on.

It was a win-win for them both. Elliott scored an ex-tennis pro for his documentary; Jared scored priceless advertising to tout the kids' rec centre he was funding to the entire country.

'So who's the lucky lady?'

Elliott glanced towards the door, his eyebrows shooting skywards.

'Here she comes now. And wow. You always were a lucky dog.'

Jared turned, curious to see who he'd be stuck with on the island. Not that he cared. He'd socialised on the tennis circuit for years, could fake it with the best of them. Easy.

But as his gaze collided with a pair of unusual blue eyes the colour of the cerulean-blue ocean of Bondi on a clear day, their accusatory gaze cutting straight through him, he knew spending a week on a deserted island with Kristi Wilde would be far from easy.

'I'll deal with you later,' Jared muttered at a confused Elliott as Kristi strutted towards the table on impossibly high heels.

She'd always had a thing for shoes, almost as much as he'd had a thing for her.

'Good to see you—'

'Did you know about this?'

Though she'd cut his intro short, she had no hope of avoiding his kiss and as he ducked down to kiss her cheek the familiarity of her sweet, spicy scent slammed into him with the power of a Nadal serve, quickly followed by a host of memories.

The exhilaration of climbing the Harbour Bridge eclipsed by a laughing, exuberant Kristi falling into his arms, and his bed later that night.

Long, sultry summer nights lingering over seafood platters at Doyles on Watson's Bay, snuggling close in a water taxi afterwards, heading back to his place, desperately trying to rein in their limited self-control.

Best of all, the easy-going, laid-back, fun-filled relationship they'd shared.

Until she'd started clinging, demanding, and he'd bolted.

With good reason. His tennis rankings had been shooting for the stars at the time, he'd had no choice but to repay the people who'd invested their time in him. He'd never wanted to be a user, someone who took their birthright for granted, like his parents.

Ironic, that what had started out as a babysitting exercise, a place the snooty Malones could offload their only child for a few hours a day, had turned into a lucrative career filled with fame, fortune and more women than any guy knew what to do with.

Strangely, only one woman had ever got close enough to see the real him, the guy behind the laid-back smile.

And he was looking straight at her.

While his career hadn't been the only reason he'd left, seeing her here, now, just as vibrant, just as beautiful, reinforced exactly how much he'd given up by walking away from her.

His lips wanted to linger, but she didn't give him time, stepping away with a haughty tilt of her head that might've worked if he hadn't seen the softening around her mouth, the flash of recognition in her eyes.

'Well? Did you know about this?'

Placing a hand in the small of her back to guide her to a chair, unsurprised when she stiffened, he shook his head.

'I just learned my partner in crime's identity in this fiasco a second before you walked through the door.'

'Fiasco is right.'

He smiled at her vehement agreement as Elliott held out his hand.

'Pleased to meet you. Elliott J. Barnaby, the producer of *Stranded*. Glad to have you on board.'

'That's what we need to discuss.'

Gesturing to a waiter, she placed an order for sparkling mineral water with lime, before squaring her shoulders, a fighting stance as familiar as the tilt of her head.

'Before we begin this discussion, let me make a few things clear. One, I'm here under sufferance. Two, I'm doing this for the money.'

She held up a finger, jabbed it in his direction. 'Three, this island better be big enough for the both of us because I'd rather swim back to the mainland than be cooped up with you for a week.'

Elliott's head swivelled between them, curiosity making his eyes gleam.

'You two know each other?'

She jerked her head in his direction. 'Didn't his lordship tell you?'

Elliott grinned. 'Tell me what?'

'We know each other,' Jared interjected calmly, well aware Elliott would want to know exactly how well they knew each other later. 'Old friends.'

Kristi muffled a snort as he shot her a wink. 'Getting reacquainted is going to be loads of fun.'

'Yeah, like getting a root canal,' she muttered, her glare mutinous.

After another dreary rehab session with Madame Lash, the physio from hell, Jared had trudged in here, ready to talk business with Elliott, not particularly caring who he'd be stuck with for a week.

Now, the thought of battling wits with a sassy, smart-mouthed Kristi for seven days brightened his morning considerably.

Struggling to keep a grin off his face, he folded his arms, faced Elliott.

'Us knowing each other shouldn't be a problem?'

Elliott shook his head. 'On the contrary, should make for some interesting interaction. The documentary is about exposing the reality behind reality TV. How you talk, react, bounce off each other, when confined for a week without other social interactions should make for good viewing.'

Elliott paused, frowned. 'Old friends? That didn't mean you lived together for any time?'

'Hell, no!'

The flicker of hurt in Kristi's memorable blue

eyes had him cursing his outburst, but in the next instant she'd tilted her chin, stared him down, making him doubt he'd glimpsed it at all.

'Cohabiting with a child isn't my idea of fun,' she said, her hauteur tempered with the challenging dare in her narrowed eyes.

She wanted him to respond, to fight back, to fire a few taunts. Well, let her wait. They had plenty of time for that. An entire seven days. Alone. With no entertainment other than each other. Interesting.

Oblivious to the tension simmering between them, Elliott rubbed his hands together.

'Good. Because that would've changed the status quo. This way, your reactions will be more genuine.'

He plucked a folder filled with documents from his pile and slid it across the table towards Kristi.

'I'm aware your boss put your name forward for this, so you need to look over all the legalities, sign the forms where asterisked, we'll go from there.'

She nodded, flipped open the folder, took the pen Elliott offered and started reading, the pen idly tapping her bottom lip. A bottom lip Jared remembered well; for its fullness, its softness, its melting heat as it moulded to his…

Having her read gave him time to study her, really study her. She'd been a cute, perky twenty-one-year-old when they'd dated, her blonde hair wild and untamed, her figure fuller, her clothes eclectic. She'd always been inherently beautiful and while her nose might be slightly larger than average, it added character to a face graced by beauty.

Now, with her perfect make-up, perfectly straight blow-dried hair, perfect streamlined body and perfect pink designer suit, she intrigued him more than ever.

He liked her tousled and ruffled and feisty, and, while her new image might be all corporate and controlled, he'd hazard a guess the old Kristi wouldn't be lurking far beneath the surface.

'All looks okay.'

She signed several documents and, with a heavy sigh, handed them to Elliott. 'Everything I need to know in here?'

Elliott nodded. 'Do you know anything about *Stranded*?'

She shook her head. 'My pushy boss didn't go into specifics.'

Jared leaned across, held his hand up to his mouth, his loud conspiratorial whisper exaggerated. 'Now you're in for it. He'll give you the hour-long spiel he gave me.'

Her mouth twitched before she returned her attention to Elliott, who was more than comfortable to elaborate on his favourite topic.

'While it's basically a competition for the prize money, which will go to the participant who nails the challenges and gains the most hits on their Internet networking sites, I want this documentary to make a social statement on our TV viewing and the way we network today.'

While her heart sank at the conditions imposed on winning the prize—she'd always been lousy at sports and no way could she beat Jared in the popularity stakes on the Net—Elliot continued.

'There's a glut of reality TV at the moment. Cooking, dating, singing, dancing, housemates, you name it, there's a reality show filming it. I want *Stranded* to be more than that. I want it to show two people interacting, without social distractions, without direct interference, without the fanfare, without judges, and see how they get along. I want honest feedback.'

She nodded, gestured to her folder. 'That's where the daily blog and Twitter updates come in?'

'Uh-huh. It'll give the public instant access to your immediate feelings, build anticipation for when I screen the documentary a week after you return. Building hype and viewer expectation makes for more interesting viewing.'

'So we're filmed all the time?'

She screwed up her nose, as enthralled with the idea as he was.

Elliott steepled his fingers like a puppet master looking forward to yanking their strings.

'No, the cameras are motion-activated, and only situated on certain parts of the island. If you want privacy or time out, there are designated areas.'

Her relief was palpable, as Jared wondered what would make her desperate enough to do this. Sure, she'd said the money, but she'd never been money-driven so there had to be more to it. Then again, it had been eight years. How well did he really know her?

It was different for him. His life had been laid out for public consumption the last seven years, what he ate, where he went, what car he drove, all open to interpretation.

He'd learned to shut off, to ignore the intrusion, was now using it to his advantage for the rec centre.

But what did she get out of this apart from a chance to win the money?

'Good to know.' Jared tapped the side of his nose, leaned towards her. 'Just in case you feel the urge to take advantage of me, you can do it off camera.'

'In your dreams, Malone.'

'There've been plenty of those, Wilde.'

To his delight, she blushed, dropped her gaze to focus on her fiddling fingers before she removed them from the table, hid them in her lap. He gave her five seconds to compose herself and, on cue, her gaze snapped to his, confident, challenging.

'You really want to do this here?' he murmured,

grateful when Elliott jerked his head towards the restrooms and made a hasty exit.

'Do what?'

She was good, all faux wide-eyed innocence and smug mouth. Well, she might be good but he was better. He'd always lobbed back every verbal volley levelled his way, had enjoyed their wordplay as much as their foreplay.

She stimulated him like no other woman he'd ever met and the thought of spending a week getting reacquainted had him as jittery as pre-Grand Slam.

'You know what.'

He leaned into her personal space, not surprised when she didn't flinch, didn't give an inch.

'You and me. Like this.' He pointed at her, him. 'The way we were.'

'Careful, you'll break into song any minute now.'

'Feeling sentimental?'

'Hardly. I'd have to care to want to take a stroll down memory lane.'

'And your point is?'

She shrugged, studied her manicured nails at arm's length.

'I don't.'

He laughed, sat back, laid an arm along the back of his chair, his fingers in tantalisingly close proximity to her shoulder.

'You always were a lousy liar.'

'I'm not—'

'There's a little twitch you get right here.' He touched a fingertip just shy of a freckle near her top lip. 'It's a dead giveaway.'

She stilled, the rebellious gleam in her eyes replaced by a flicker of fear before she blinked, erasing any hint of vulnerability with a bat of her long eyelashes. 'Still delusional, I see. Must be all the whacks on the head with tennis balls.'

'I don't miss-hit.'

'Not what I've seen.'

'Ah, nice to know you've been keeping an eye on my career.'

'Hard to miss when your publicity-hungry mug is plastered everywhere I look.'

She paused, her defiance edged with curiosity. 'Is that why you're doing this? Publicity for your comeback?'

'I'm not making a comeback.'

The familiar twist low in his gut made a mockery of his adamant stance that it didn't matter.

He'd fielded countless questions from the media over the last year, had made his decision, had scheduled a press conference. And while he'd reconciled with his decision months ago the thought of leaving his career behind, turning his back on the talent that had saved him, niggled.

Tennis had been his escape, his goal, his saviour, all rolled into one. While he'd originally resented being dumped at the local tennis club by his narcissistic parents, he'd soon found a solitude there he rarely found elsewhere.

He'd been good, damn good, and soon the attention of the coaches, the talent scouts, had made him want to work harder, longer, honing his skill with relentless drive.

He'd had a goal in mind. Get out of Melbourne, away from his parents and their bickering, drinking and unhealthy self-absorption.

It had worked. Tennis had saved him.

And, while resigned to leaving it behind, a small part of him was scared, petrified in fact, of letting go of the only thing that had brought normality to his life.

'You're retiring?'

'That's the plan.'

He glanced at his watch, wishing Elliott would reappear. Trading banter with Kristi was one thing, fielding her curiosity about his retirement another.

'Why?'

Her gaze, pinpoint sharp, bored into him the same way it always did when she knew he was being evasive.

He shrugged, leaned back, shoved his hands in

his pockets to stop them from rearranging cutlery and giving away his forced casual posture.

'My knee's blown.'

Her eyes narrowed; she wasn't buying his excuse. 'Reconstructed, I heard. Happens to athletes all the time. So what's the real reason?'

He needed to give her something or she'd never let up. He'd seen her like this before: harassing him to reveal a surprise present, pestering him to divulge the whereabouts of their surprise weekend away. She was relentless when piqued and there was no way he'd sit here and discuss his real reasons with her.

'The hunger's gone. I'm too old to match it with the up-and-coming youngsters.'

'What are you, all of thirty?'

'Thirty-one.'

'But surely some tennis champions played 'til they were—?'

'Leave it!'

He regretted his outburst the instant the words left his mouth, her curiosity now rampant rather than appeased.

Rubbing his chin, he said, 'I'm going to miss it but I've got other things I want to do with my life so don't go feeling sorry for me.'

'Who said anything about feeling sorry for you?' The relaxing of her thinned lips belied her response. 'You'd be the last guy to pity, what with your jet-set lifestyle, your homes in Florida, Monte Carlo and Sydney. Your luxury car collection. Your—'

'You read too many tabloids,' he muttered, recognising the irony with him ready to capitalise on the paparazzi's annoying scrutiny of his life to boost the rec centre's profile into the stratosphere.

'Part of my job.'

He laughed. 'Bull. You used to love poring over those gossip rags for the hell of it.'

'Research, I tell you.'

She managed a tight smile and it struck him how good this felt: the shared memories, the familiarity. He knew her faults, she knew his and where that closeness had once sent him bolting, he now found it strangely intriguing.

'We need to get together before we leave for Lorikeet Island.'

Her smile faded, replaced by wariness. 'Why?'

'For old times' sake.'

He leaned closer, crooked his finger at her. 'Surely you don't want to rehash our history in front of the cameras?'

With a toss of her hair, she sipped at her mineral water, glancing at him over the rim.

'The only thing happening in front of the cameras is me pretending to like you.'

Laying a hand on her forearm, pleased when she stiffened in awareness, he murmured, 'Sure you need to pretend? Because I remember a time when—'

'Okay, okay, I liked you.'

She snatched her arm away, but not before he'd seen the responsive glimmer darkening her eyes to sapphire. 'It was a phase in my early twenties that passed along with my passion for leg warmers and spiral perms.'

Not backing off an inch, he shifted his chair closer to hers.

'Didn't you hear? Leg warmers are making a comeback.'

'You aren't.'

Her stricken expression showed him exactly how much she still cared despite protestations to the contrary. 'With me, I meant. Not your career. Sorry. Damn…'

'It's okay.'

Her discomfort, while rare, was refreshing. 'So, about our pre-island catch up?'

She sighed. 'I guess it makes sense.'

'Eight, tonight?'

'Fine. Where?'

Not ready to divulge all his secrets just yet, he said, 'You'll find out.'

CHAPTER THREE

Stranded *Survival Tip #3*
Pack all your troubles in your old kit bag; but
don't forget protection…just in case.

'YOU owe me an ice cream for making me wait
in the car.'

Kristi grabbed Meg's arm and dragged her away
from the all-seeing front window of Icebergs. 'You
weren't in the car, you were strolling on the beach.'

'How do you know?'

'Because I saw you craning your neck to get a
squiz at Jared and me through the window.'

'I wasn't craning. I was trying to stand on
tiptoe.' Meg shook her head, disgusted. 'Still
couldn't see a darn thing.'

Perking up as they neared the ice-cream stand,
Meg grinned. 'So, is he still as gorgeous in real
life as all those dishy pictures in the papers?'

'Better,' Kristi admitted reluctantly, her head
still reeling with the impact of twenty minutes in

Jared's intoxicating company, her body buzzing with recognition.

She hadn't expected such an instantaneous, in-your-face, overwhelming awareness of what they'd once shared, the memories bombarding her as fast as his quips.

Every time he looked at her, she remembered staring into each other's eyes over fish and chips on Manly beach.

Every time he laughed, she remembered their constant teasing and the resultant chuckles.

Every time he'd touched her, she remembered, in slow, exquisite detail, how he'd played her body with skill and expertise, heat flowing strong and swiftly to every inch of her.

'I could strangle Ros for putting me in this position.'

'And which position would that be? Stranded on an island with Jared? Or maybe back in his arms or—'

Kristi gave her sister a narrowed look.

'If Ros hadn't dangled the promotion, I never would've gone through with this.'

'Even for a chance to win a hundred grand?'

'Even for that.'

A lie, but she didn't want to tip Meg off to her plans for the prize money. Her little sister hated pity, hated charity worse.

When her no-good son-of-a-gun fiancé fled upon hearing news of her pregnancy, it wasn't enough he took her self-respect, her trust, her hopes and dreams of an amazing marriage like their parents had shared.

Oh, no, the low-life scumbag had to take every last cent of her money too, leaving Meg living in a one-bedroom hellhole in the middle of gangland Sydney, footing bills for their cancelled wedding and working two jobs to save enough money to take a few months off after the baby was born.

Life sucked for her pragmatic sister and, while Meg pretended to be upbeat for the sake of the adorable little Prue, she couldn't hide the dark rings of fatigue circling her eyes or the wary glances she darted if any guy got too close.

Trusting the wrong guy had shattered Meg's dreams, her vivacity, her hope for a brilliant future, and Kristi would do anything—including being holed up with her ex for a week—to bring the sparkle back to her sister's eyes.

'What are you going to do with the moula if you win?'

'You'll find out.'

Stopping at the ice-cream stand, Kristi placed an order for two whippy cones with the lot, her gaze drifting back to Icebergs.

She'd left Jared sitting there, all tanned, toned,

six four of tennis star in his prime. He'd always been sexy in that bronze, outdoorsy, ruffled way many Aussie males were, but the young guy she'd lusted after wasn't a patch on the older, mature Jared.

Years playing in the sun had deepened his skin to mahogany, adding character lines to a handsome face, laugh lines around his eyes. He'd always had those, what with his penchant for laughter.

Nothing had fazed Jared; he was rarely serious. Unfortunately, that had included getting serious about a relationship, resulting in him walking away from her to chase his precious career.

He'd been on the cusp of greatness back then, had vindicated his choice by winning Wimbledon, the French Open and the US Open, twice. The Australian Open had been the only tournament to elude the great Jared Malone for the first few years of his illustrious career and she'd often pondered his apparent distraction in exiting the first or second round of the Melbourne-based tournament.

The ensuing pictures of him with some blonde bombshell or busty brunette on his arm went a long way to explaining his early departures and she gritted her teeth against the fact she'd cared.

Not any more.

She'd seen the evidence firsthand of what choosing the wrong man to spend your life with could do and, considering Jared had run rather than build a future with her, he had proved he wasn't the man for her.

'Your ice cream's melting.'

Blinking, Kristi paid, handed Meg her cone and headed for the sand.

'You're walking down there in those?'

Meg pointed at her favourite Louboutin hot pink patent shoes with the staggering heel.

'Sheesh, hooking up with tennis boy again must really have you rattled.'

'I'm not "hooking up" with anybody, I'm just going to sit on the wall, take a breather before heading back to work.'

Meg licked her ice cream, her suspicious stare not leaving her sister's face.

'You two used to date. Stands to reason there *is* a fair chance of you hooking up again on that deserted island.'

'Shut up and eat your ice cream.'

They sat in companionable silence, Kristi determinedly ignoring Meg's logic. The sharp sun, refreshing ocean breeze, packed beach were reminiscent of countless other days they'd done this together as youngsters and, later, bonded in their grief over their parents' premature death.

While their parents might have left them financially barren, they could thank them for a family

closeness that had always been paramount, ahead
of everything else.

'What do you really think about all this, Megs?'

Crunching the last of her cone, Meg tilted her
face up to the sun.

'Honestly? You've never got over tennis boy.'

'That's bull. I've been engaged twice!'

Meg sat up, tapped her ring finger.

'Yet you're not married. Interesting.'

Indignant, Kristi tossed the rest of her ice cream
in the bin, folded her arms.

'So I made wrong decisions? Better I realised
before traipsing up the aisle.'

Meg held up her hands. 'Hey, you'll get no arguments from me on that point. Look at the farcical
mess my short-lived engagement turned into.'

A shadow passed over her sister's face as Kristi
silently cursed her blundering insensitivity.

'Forget I asked—'

Meg made a zipping motion over her lips as she
continued. 'But Avery and Barton were both
decent guys and you seemed happy. Yet the closer
the wedding got both times, the more emotionally
remote you were. Why's that?'

Because she'd been chasing a dream each time,
a dream she'd had since a little girl, a dream of the
perfect wedding.

The dress, the flowers, the reception, she

could see it all so clearly, had saved pictures in a scrapbook.

What she couldn't see was the groom—discounting the magazine pic of Jared Meg had pasted there as a joke when they'd been dating—and while Avery and Barton had momentarily superimposed their images in her dream, they ultimately hadn't fit.

Avery had entered her life six months after her parents died, had been supportive and gracious and non-pressuring. She'd been lost, grieving and he'd helped her, providing security at a time she needed it most.

It had taken her less than four months to figure out their engagement was a by-product of her need for stability after her parents' death and she'd ended it.

Not that she'd learned.

Barton had been a friend, supportive of her break up and the loss of her parents, so supportive it had seemed natural to slip into a relationship eight months after Avery had gone.

While their engagement had lasted longer, almost a year, she'd known it wasn't right deep down, where she craved a unique love-of-her-life romance, not a comfortable relationship that left her warm and fuzzy without a spark in sight.

She'd been guilt-ridden for months after ending

both engagements, knowing she shouldn't have let the relationships go so far but needing to hold onto her dream, needing to feel safe and treasured and loved after the world as she knew it had changed.

Her family had made her feel protected and when she'd lost that she'd looked for security elsewhere. She just wished she hadn't hurt Avery and Barton in the process.

'You know why you really didn't go through with those weddings. It could do you good to admit it.'

Meg nudged her and she bumped right back. She knew what Meg was implying; after Jared, no man had lived up to expectations.

While she'd briefly contemplated that reasoning after each break-up, she'd dismissed it. Jared had been so long ago, had never entertained the possibility of a full-blown relationship let alone a lifetime commitment and he'd never fit in her happily ever after scenario.

Liar. Remember the day he walked in on you in your room-mate's wedding dress while she was away on her honeymoon? The day you joked about it being their turn soon?

Not only had she envisioned him as her perfect groom, she'd almost believed it for those six months they'd dated.

Until he'd dumped her and bolted without a backward glance.

'I guess the closer the weddings came on both occasions, the more I realised Avery and Barton didn't really know me. Sure, we shared similar interests, moved in similar social circles, had similar goals but it was just too...too...'

'Trite.'

'Perfect...' she shook her head, the familiar confusion clouding her brain when she tried to fathom her reasons for calling off her much-desired weddings. '...yet it wasn't perfect. It was like I had this vision of what I wanted and I was doing my damnedest to make it fit. Does that make sense?'

'Uh-huh.'

Meg paused, squinted her eyes in the Icebergs' direction. 'So where does tennis boy fit into your idea of perfection?'

'Malone's far from perfect.'

As the words tripped from her tongue an instant image of his sexy smile, the teasing twinkle in his eyes, the hard, ripped body, flashed across her mind, taunting her, mocking her.

Crunching loudly on the tip of her ice-cream cone, Meg sat up, dusted off her hands.

'You need to do this.'

When Kristi opened her mouth to respond, Meg held up a finger. 'Not just for the promotion or the possibility of winning all that cash. But for the chance to confront tennis boy, finally get some closure.'

The instant denial they'd had closure eight years ago died on her lips.

He'd walked in on her in that dress, had reneged on their dinner plans and avoided her calls afterwards. Except to call her from the airport before boarding his plane for Florida; and she preferred to forget what had transpired during that gem of a phone call.

Meg was right. While the promotion and prize money were huge incentives to spend a week with Jared stranded on an island, getting closure was the clincher.

Standing, Kristi shot Meg a rueful smile. 'Remind me never to ask for your advice again.'

'Don't ask if you don't want to hear the truth.'

That was what scared Kristi the most. In confronting Jared, would she finally learn the truth?

About what really went wrong in their relationship all those years ago?

Elliott ordered another double-shot espresso, slid his wire-rimmed glasses back on, peered over them.

'What gives between you and Kristi Wilde? I've never heard you mention her.'

Jared dismissed Elliott's curiosity with a wave of his hand.

'Old history.'

'A history I have a feeling I need to know before we get this project underway.'

Elliott tapped his stack of documents. 'There were enough sparks flying between the two of you to set this lot alight and I don't want anything threatening to scuttle this documentary before it's off the ground. So what's the story?'

'I met her when I first moved to Sydney. Spent a few months hanging out, having fun, before I headed for training camp at Florida. That's it.'

'All sounds very simple and uncomplicated.'

'It is.'

Jared downed a glass of water before he was tempted to tell Elliott the rest.

The way she was totally unlike any of the women in his usual social circle back in Melbourne. Her lack of pretence, lack of artificialities, lack of cunning. The way she used to look at him, with laughter and warmth and genuine admiration in her eyes. The way she made him feel, as if he didn't have a care in the world and didn't have the responsibility of living up to expectation hanging around his neck like a stone.

No, he couldn't tell his mate any of that, for voicing his trip down memory lane might catapult him right back to a place he'd rather not be: hurting a woman he cared about.

Elliott rested his folded arms on the table, leaned forward with a shake of his head.

'Only problem is, my friend, I know you, and simple and uncomplicated are not words I'd use to describe you or any of your relationships.'

'It wasn't a relationship,' he said, an uneasy stab making a mockery of that.

While they'd never spelled it out as such, they'd spent every spare moment in each other's company, had spent every night together, had painted this city red, blue, white and any other damn colour, and belittling what they had to assuage his friend's curiosity didn't sit well with him.

'Then what was it?'

The best time of his life.

The first woman he'd ever been involved with.

The first person he'd allowed close enough to care.

The first time he'd allowed himself to feel anything other than caution and judgement and bitterness.

He'd been numb after escaping his parents' bizarre turnaround when they suddenly started acknowledging he existed, had been driven to succeed, to utilise the talent he'd uncovered through their neglect.

Melbourne had held nothing but bad memories and newly clinging parents for him and moving to Sydney had been as much about fresh starts as fostering his career.

Though she hadn't known it at the time, Kristi had been a saviour: a friend, a lover, a distraction, all rolled into one.

And when she'd got too close…well, he'd done the only thing he could.

He'd run.

'Kristi and I dated casually. We had fun.'

'And you didn't break her heart?'

He hadn't stuck around long enough for that; had made sure of it.

'Would she be taking part in your little social experiment if I had?'

Apparently satisfied, Elliott nodded, his glasses sliding down his nose as he absent-mindedly pushed them back up.

'Good point. She seemed feisty. I reckon she would've skewered you if you'd done a number on her.'

'Too right.'

Not that he agreed with his friend's assessment. Back then, Kristi had had vulnerability written all over her. She'd acted as if she didn't care but he'd seen the signs, had caught the unguarded longing stares she'd cast him when she thought he wasn't looking.

Then there was that bridal shower she'd been

so hyped about, throwing a huge shindig at her apartment for her room-mate, her incessant chatter of gowns and registries and invitations sending a shudder through him.

Marriage was never on the cards for him and just being close to all that hearts and flowers crap made his gut roil.

Then he'd walked in on her one day, standing in front of a cheval mirror, wearing a shiny white wedding gown and a beatific smile. If that vision hadn't sent a ripple of horror through him, her words had.

'It'll be our turn next.'

Not a hope in Hades.

So he'd pulled back, brought forward his departure date to a Florida training camp, said goodbye with a phone call. He'd taken the coward's way out but, the way he saw it, he'd made the right decision.

He'd never promised Kristi anything, had made it clear from the start their dating had a time limit. Wasn't his fault she'd interpreted it as anything other than what it was: a casual fling, fun while it lasted.

'If you two parted amicably, does that mean you're going to pick up where you left off on the island?'

'For your nosy viewers to see? Not likely.'

As the words tumbled easily he had to admit he'd wondered the same thing himself, the thought crossing his mind the instant she'd strutted in here with her shoulders squared for battle and her eyes flashing fire.

'Too bad. Would've been nice to add a little romance to the mix.'

With a shake of his head, Jared stood. 'You're a sap.'

'No, I'm a producer after ratings.'

Throwing a few notes on the table, Elliott hoisted his load into his arms and stood too.

'And sex sells, my friend.'

Jared grunted in response, a certain part of him agreeing with Elliott, with the faintest hope Kristi would too.

CHAPTER FOUR

Stranded *Survival Tip #4*
*They're playing our song. Pity it's the theme
song from* Titanic.

As KRISTI spritzed her custom-made patchouli
perfume behind her ears, on her pulse points, her
hand shook, the infernal buzz of nerves in her
tummy hard to subdue.

No matter how many times she mentally recited
tonight was about fine-tuning details for their
week on Lorikeet Island, she couldn't ignore the
fact catching up with Jared reeked of a date.

She didn't want to think of it as a date. A date
implied intimacy and excitement and expectation,
feelings she'd given up on a long time ago where
he was concerned.

Jared Malone might have once rocked her
world, but she'd got over it. He could flash that
sexy smile and charm her with witty wordplay all
he liked, it wouldn't change a thing.

She'd seen the way he'd looked at her during their brief meeting at Icebergs; as if he remembered everything about her and would love to take a fast sprint down memory lane.

If he tried, she had four words for him.

Not in this lifetime.

Leaning into the mirror, she tilted her head to one side to fasten an earring. The long, straight silver spiral shimmered as she turned, caught the light, reflected, matching her sequinned halter top perfectly.

She loved the top's funkiness, had offset it with low-slung black hipster formal pants. Chic, without trying too hard. Not that she'd dithered too long on her wardrobe choice. She wanted to speed through this evening, speed through the seven interminably long days on the island and regain equilibrium.

For while she might not have feelings for Jared any more, seeing him again had her on edge, a strange combination of anger, fear and reservation. While he could act as if things hadn't ended badly between them, she couldn't, unable to shake the foreboding that the longer she spent in his company, the more chance she had of making a fool of herself again.

For that was exactly what she'd done last time around.

Made an A-grade ass of herself.

She'd known he'd had to leave eventually, yet had started to cling the closer his departure grew, culminating in that silly, angry ultimatum during their last phone call.

She'd made him choose. Her or tennis. How young and stupid had she been?

When he'd walked in on her in that wedding dress the week before he left, she'd been glad. She'd wanted him to see how she looked, wanted him to envisage the dream of happily-ever-after as much as she wanted it.

So she'd made that flyaway comment about it being their turn next, half hoping he'd sweep her into his arms and take her with him.

Instead, he'd withdrawn, closed off, the last week before he departed, leaving her morose, desperate and hurt, incredibly hurt.

Her ridiculous ultimatum had been born of anger and resentment and rejection, something she should never have done.

But she couldn't change the past; the memory of her naivety made her cringe and seeing Jared again only served to resurrect those old feelings of embarrassment and mortification.

He'd appeared unfazed by their past while she'd sat through their meeting mentally kicking herself all over again.

Now she had to spend a week on a deserted island with him.

Her humiliation was complete.

The intercom buzzed and with one, last quick glance in the mirror she trudged across the room, grateful her platform T-bar metallic sandals only allowed her to move at a snail's pace, and hit the button to let him in downstairs.

She'd wondered if he'd call her at work to get the address, surprised when he hadn't. It meant he remembered, leading to the next obvious question: what else did he remember?

Much to her chagrin, she hadn't forgotten a thing about him.

Avery's shoe size? Erased from her memory banks for ever.

Barton's preferred margarine? Gone.

Yet she could recall in startling clarity how Jared liked his eggs—poached; his coffee—white with one; his side of the bed—right.

Maybe that had been half the problem with both engagements? The guys had been fine, upstanding citizens with good jobs, good looks and good credentials, but they weren't Jared.

The thought had crossed her mind both times she'd broken off the engagements but she'd dismissed it as a young girl's whimsical memory of a brief romance that had been too good to be true.

She'd had genuine feelings for both fiancés, had gone through her version of grieving both times: intermittent crying jags, locked away at home for a week, consumed copious tubs of her favourite Turkish delight ice cream.

She'd pondered their relationships at length, had tried to erase the final departure from both engagements each time: the shock, the bewilderment from the guys, the guilt, the sadness from her.

It had taken her a while to recover from Avery, then Barton, and each time she'd started reminiscing about Jared and hated herself for it.

The girls at work discussed their first loves all the time: the thrill, the newness, the heady sensation of being on heightened awareness every second of every day, how it all faded.

That was the problem. The buzz between her and Jared hadn't had a chance to fade. He'd absconded before the gloss had worn off, left her embarrassed she'd read so much into their relationship, furious how he'd ended it yet pathetically pining when he hadn't looked back.

The memory of their parting doused any simmer of sentimentality she might have felt towards this meeting, annoyance replacing her memories as she yanked open the door.

'Good. You're here. Let's go.'

Her brusqueness evaporated when she saw him

leaning against the jamb, wearing a wicked grin that made her facial muscles twitch in eagerness to respond.

'Wow.'

She stiffened as his appreciative gaze roved over her freely, the naughty twinkle in his eyes undermining her as much as that damn smile.

Ignoring the responding quiver in her knees, she dropped her gaze, discovering his designer loafers, dark denim, and cotton shirt the colour of her favourite butterscotch didn't help re-establish her immunity.

He'd always been a great dresser, could wear anything and make it look like haute couture. Yet another thing she'd loved about him. A love that meant jack considering how fast he'd run.

'You ready to go?'

Scanning her face for a reason behind her snippiness, he chuckled, held out his hand. 'Shall we?'

Ignoring his hand, she nodded, needing to wipe that twinkle from his eye, to establish she wouldn't engage in whatever game he intended for tonight.

'If you're planning on flirting your way through dinner, forget it. I'm doing this so we get everything straight before we're stuck on the island. Understand?'

His mock salute and wide grin spoke volumes:

he'd do as he damned well pleased tonight, regardless.

'Perfectly.'

She shook her head, frowned. 'I mean it. I'm immune so don't waste your breath—'

'Did it ever strike you I'm uncomfortable about all this and flirting is the only way I know how to ease back into how we were before?'

His honesty surprised her, for, while his tone was light-hearted, she saw the flicker of uncertainty in his eyes.

A sliver of guilt penetrated her prickly armour. If she was feeling uncomfortable about this whole scenario, why shouldn't he?

'We can't go back to how it was before.'

His answering smile elicited a twinge of remembrance, a yearning to do just that.

'We laughed a lot back then, were easy in each other's company. Wouldn't it be great to recapture some of that on the island, especially in front of the cameras?'

Of course, that was what this was about: re-establishing some kind of rapport so they didn't embarrass themselves on camera. She should've known, but for a split second she'd almost wished he were flirting with her because he wanted to recreate some of the other magic they'd shared back then.

'I guess you're right.'

'That's my girl.'

She wasn't, had never been really.

Maybe Jared could ignore the past, could don his smooth, funny, adorable persona and hope she'd forget how things had ended between them, but she had as much hope of that as scaling the Opera House in her favourite four-inch Louboutin's.

Hurt faded but it wasn't forgotten.

Not when the man who'd broken her heart would be in her face for the next week.

Grateful he hadn't chosen any of their old haunts, Kristi stepped through the enormous glass door of Sydney's newest East meets West fusion restaurant and nodded her thanks at Jared. Another thing that hadn't changed about him: his impeccable manners.

'Have you been here before?'

She shook her head, tried not to look suitably impressed as she glanced around at the soaring ceilings, steel beams and enough chrome and glass to build an entire suburb.

'Rumour has it you have to be the prime minister or an Oscar winner to get a booking for the next year.'

She paused, quirked an eyebrow. 'Or apparently a star tennis player?'

Chuckling, he tapped the side of his nose. 'It's not what you know, it's who you know.'

'Obviously.'

She swanned through the restaurant, aware of the not too subtle envious glances cast their way. Not that she could blame the women.

Jared Malone, world-renowned playboy, was a serious babe.

Voted number one sexiest sportsman for three years running in all the top women's magazines.

Not that she'd kept count. Flicking through glossies was a fabulous part of her job, keeping abreast of the latest PR strategies, and while she'd quickly flipped over pages wherever Jared appeared she'd still noticed.

Any woman with a pulse would have to be half dead not to notice him.

And she'd be stuck with him, on a deserted island, for a week. Gain a promotion out of it. Possibly win a hundred grand. So why the reservations?

As they reached the table, his hand guiding her in the small of her back, his breath the barest whisper against her heated skin, she knew exactly why she wasn't doing cartwheels over the next week.

It would've been bad enough spending seven days on an island with some stranger, but a week with a guy she'd once loved, who knew her weaknesses, who knew her intimately?

Heck.

'You're nervous.'

She feigned ignorance as he held out her chair and she sat, grateful for the support when his hand grazed the back of her neck, a particularly sensitive spot as well he knew.

'About our little island jaunt.'

She winced. 'It shows?'

Chuckling, he ran a fingertip just above her top lip. 'You get this little wrinkle right about here when you think too much.'

Brushing his hand away, she gulped from the crystal water glass thankfully filled to the brim.

'Aren't you the slightest bit uncomfortable about all this?

He sat back, folded his arms, that familiar cocky grin making her heart jive and jump and jitterbug.

'No.'

'So it doesn't matter we had…'

'A past?'

His grin widened. 'Surely you'd rather be stuck on Lorikeet Island with me than some stranger?'

She'd debated the fact, hadn't reached any conclusions yet. She could've been distantly polite with a stranger, could've faked enthusiasm for the documentary, could've been totally and utterly uninvolved.

Spending a week with Jared, just the two of them, would render it impossible to stay distant.

She knew so much about this man, remembered details she should've forgotten: how he bounced out of bed every morning and stretched five times, how he hated orange but loved mango juice, how he made adorable little snoring/snuffling sounds when asleep after an exhausting game.

How he devoured sushi like a man starved, how he preferred swimming in the ocean to a swimming pool, how he liked sporting magazines over novels.

So many memories, all of them good. Except the one where he walked away from her without a backward glance.

'If you have to think that long, maybe I've lost my charm.'

She rolled her eyes. 'Nothing wrong with your charm and you darn well know it.'

He wiped his brow. 'Phew, for a second there you had me worried.'

When he'd left, she'd missed many things, his sense of humour being one of them. They'd always sparred like this, swapping banter along with huge chunks of their lives. She'd loved it, loved him.

Which brought her full circle back to her original dilemma: how dangerous would it be being stuck on an island with Jared?

Her sorrow at their break-up and any residual humiliation should ensure immunity to him after all this time. She'd moved on since, had two engagements to prove it.

Broken engagements, her insidiously annoying voice of reason whispered.

Guys she'd fallen for enough to think she wanted to marry, just not enough to take that final step and actually say, 'I do.' She'd loved both Avery and Barton, loved their gentleness and patience and understanding. They'd reminded her of her high-school boyfriends, the nice guys who'd carry her books and write corny love letters and give her a lift on the handlebars of their bikes.

She'd been horrid to those boys, demanding and snooty and condescending, thrilled to have their attention yet secretly craving the Prince Charmings she read about in her mum's romance novels.

Thankfully, she'd grown up enough to treat her men better, but a small part of her wondered if she didn't end up treating her fiancés as badly in the end.

Yes, she'd definitely moved on from Jared, couldn't have loved those men if deep down in her heart she secretly pined for her first love. Besides, he'd shattered her grand illusions of loving him by choosing his career over her, by not being willing to work out a compromise.

She'd worked through the stages of grief after he'd left: anger, denial, reaching acceptance months later.

Simply, he hadn't loved her.

Yet sitting across from him, in all his confident, laid-back, gorgeous glory, she had a hard time shaking the memories of how it had once been.

Ignoring the nervous churning in her gut, she grabbed a menu and stuck it up, using it as a barrier to hide her readable face, not willing to let him know the turmoil within.

'Shall we order? I'm famished.'

'I took the liberty of ordering the eight-course degustation menu.'

He signalled to a waiter, who instantly bore down on them brandishing an expensive bottle of champagne. 'That way we get to sample a bit of everything. Hope you don't mind?'

Normally she wouldn't but seeing him assume the old role of 'man of the world', a guy who'd been around the block a time or two in comparison to her naivety back then, grated. But what was the point of stirring up trouble? Once their week together was over, she'd go her way, he'd go his. He was an expert at that.

'Fine.'

As the waiter poured the champagne she took the opportunity to glance around. Not surprisingly, every woman within a few feet cast surreptitious peeks at Jared when their partners weren't watching, their eyes predatory until they slid to her, when their gleam became curious, envious.

She'd never had to deal with that before, would've hated it. Working in PR, she'd mingled with the rich and famous, had seen high-profile relationships up close and personal, and had never figured out how the women put up with their partners being fawned over by other women; or, worse, blatantly propositioned.

She would never tolerate it. Thankfully, she would never have to.

'What are you looking at?'

She picked up her champagne flute, raised it in a silent toast.

'All the women around us are making goo eyes at you.'

'Where?'

He looked over his shoulder, caught a woman's eye, winked and smiled as she ducked her head and blushed.

'Oh, you mean her.'

'And her.'

She nodded to the left. 'And her.'

She jerked her head to the right. 'And her.'

'That one's behind you. How can you tell?'

With a wry grin, she raised her glass again.

'Because she's human and female and as smitten as the rest of this room with your presence.'

A corner of his mouth kicked up in that quirky smile she loved as he folded his hands on the table, leaned forward.

'Does that include you?'

She made a loud scoffing noise that descended into an embarrassing snort.

'Do I look like I'm smitten?'

Leaning even closer, so close she could smell his clean lime aftershave, see the familiar green flecks in his hazel eyes, he touched her hand.

'You look incredible, more beautiful than you were eight years ago if that's possible.'

'Been working on those lines?'

Unperturbed, he sat back, resumed his casual relaxed pose, one hand slung across the back of his chair.

'According to you, I don't need lines. Apparently women are smitten just sitting here.'

She made a rude noise that had him laughing as he picked up his champagne flute, touched it to hers.

'To us. And making the most of our island jaunt.'

'To us.'

As she echoed his toast her reservations took a serious hit as a sliver of anticipation lodged where she feared it most.

Her heart.

He took a long sip of his champagne, his eyes not leaving hers, the intensity of his stare making her increasingly uncomfortable.

Lowering his glass, he placed it on the table, leaned forward. 'You know, I was once crazy about you.'

'Yeah, so crazy you moved to the other side of the world to get away from me.'

The heat faded, his eyes instantly guarded.

'My career was taking off. You know that.'

The old familiar resentment bubbled to the surface, obliterating the unexpected joy she'd experienced just by being here, sharing a meal with him.

She had known it but had let herself get caught up in their whirlwind romance anyway. Jared had lived in the moment, wanted instant gratification, didn't want to look too far ahead, whereas she'd had enough dreams for the both of them.

Not that it had mattered. Nothing she could've said or done back then would've changed the outcome.

'Yeah, I know.'

When she wouldn't meet his gaze, he captured her hand, reluctantly releasing it when she tugged hard.

'You sound bitter.'

'You don't think I have a right to be?'

'You knew the score. I never made any promises.'

'Beyond a few months of fun?'

She snapped her fingers. 'Silly me for reading more into us spending every spare second together.'

He shook his head. 'You really want to rehash all this now? Right before we spend a week together in front of the cameras?'

What she wanted was an apology.

What she wanted was some small indication she'd meant half as much to him as he'd meant to her.

What she wanted was to annihilate the crazy, excited buzz deep in her belly that made a mockery of her indignation.

Blowing out an exasperated puff of air, she shook her head.

'No point. Let's leave the past in the past.'

His crooked smile, so familiar, so heart-rending, made a serious dent in her residual animosity.

'Look, I know this is awkward. We were great together 'til that last week, when we both acted a little crazy.'

'You think?'

He laughed and she managed a tight smile. She didn't want to discuss her humiliating ultimatum, how she'd shrieked at him, filled with hurt and anger and resentment. Crazy? She'd acted like a certified lunatic so yeah, this was beyond awkward.

'We were both young, we had different agendas.

How about we put all that behind us and try to be friends for the next week?'

Friends. Yeah, she could do friends at a pinch.

Think of the money...think of Meg and Prue...

Unfortunately, all she could think about was exactly how friendly Jared wanted to get on the island.

'Friends,' she said, gulping at her champagne, though it did little to quell her nerves as he held out his hand and, this time, she had no option but to place her hand in his and shake on it.

A simple arrangement, friends for a week.

Pity complication was her middle name.

CHAPTER FIVE

Stranded *Survival Tip #5*
When asked, 'Do you like me?' don't answer,
'I'm here, aren't I?'

FOOTFALLS scuffing the corridor outside his door grabbed Jared's attention as he wrapped up final negotiations for a popular rock band to play at Activate's official opening.

A few local kids had been dropping by since he'd opened the doors a month ago, but not enough for his liking. He still saw them loitering in small gangs on the streets, in the parks, bored, on edge, looking for trouble.

While the original idea for the centre had come to him in rehab, surrounded by partially disabled kids who needed a place to hang out, once he'd investigated sites and discovered the startling number of kids loitering on Sydney's streets he'd known his dream needed expanding.

Through months of painful, monotonous rehab,

he'd planned Activate from the ground up, investing an exorbitant sum, determined to give something back to those who needed it the most.

While his parents had been AWOL from the time he could walk, he'd never wanted for anything, their wealth a cushion against the harsher side of life.

From what he'd seen these past few months around Kings Cross, a lot of local kids needed that kind of shield.

So the centre had grown, catering for all disadvantaged kids, physically and emotionally. He'd keep the money coming, grab the free publicity from Elliott, then move on to his next venture. Whatever that was.

'Got a minute?'

He raised his head at the sound of a hesitant voice, tried to place the red-haired kid with enough facial piercings to rival his freckles, and remembered his name after a quick mental rummage.

'Sure, come in, Bluey.'

The flash of surprise in the kid's eyes, along with a quick nod of acknowledgment, vindicated the time he'd spent at the centre. He might only be financing the venture, but if his presence encouraged drop-ins for the simple fact they recognised him from tennis it was time well spent.

The kid slouched across the room, flopped into the chair.

'What can I do for you?'

Bluey picked at a hole in his jeans, plucked at the frayed edges, concentrating on his fiddling rather than looking up.

'Word on the street is you're planning on keeping this joint open day and night. That true?'

'Uh-huh.'

'Why?'

Bluey's head snapped up, fear mixed with mistrust in the furtive shadows clouding his eyes.

'What do you get out of it? You're just some hotshot tennis jock. Why do you care?'

'Because I do.'

A lousy response but what could he say?

He had no idea what it was like to semi-doze on a park bench, night after night, so tired you could fall into a coma, too terrified to sleep for fear of any number of horrors nabbing you.

He didn't understand the pinch of hunger, the hollow, scraping feeling in one's gut that made Dumpster leftovers an appealing feast after a while.

But he sure as hell recognised the fear in this kid's eyes, the lonely emptiness inside that no one gave a damn about you.

He might have had everything money could buy and parents only too happy to splash their cash around, but he'd lived with that same emptiness every day growing up, wishing for acknowledgement, willing them to show some semblance of sentiment rather than treating him as if he were a nobody, as if he didn't exist.

So did he care?

Hell, yeah, but how to get that across to a kid who viewed him as just another adult he couldn't trust?

'This place is here if you want it. Tell your mates. No pressure, no expectations. Just a place to hang out, play some sport.'

Bluey shrugged, resumed picking at his frayed edges. 'Chill, man. Just wondering, that's all.'

Jared couldn't tell the kid's age. Twelve? Fourteen? With his slight build, hunched shoulders, grimy face, he could've been any number of kids that frequented the Kings Cross area.

While his slashed cheekbones highlighted a gauntness honed by hunger, there was resilience about the boy, a toughness that defied anyone to pity him.

That was when it hit him.

Bluey reminded him of himself.

Fierce, determined, resentful, he'd been all that and more before he'd discovered tennis, when being the best at a sport had given him an outlet for his bitterness.

Where would Bluey end up with a little help?

It reinforced he was doing the right thing, investing in this place. Now all he had to do was tell the world about it, and that was exactly what he'd do, starting tomorrow, first day on the island.

'Do you network on the web?'

Bluey glanced up again, curious. 'Like Facebook and MySpace and stuff?'

'Yeah.'

Bluey sent him an 'are you for real?' sneer. ''Course. A few dudes have mobile phones. We get to check stuff out.'

'Good. Make sure you spread the word about this place. And keep an eye on Twitter and a blog I've set up.'

At last, a flash of recognition, of interest, reinforcing he was doing the right thing in taking part in *Stranded*. The kids would definitely sit up and take notice now.

'Yeah, whatever.'

Apparently Bluey had said what he'd come to say because he unfolded his lanky limbs from the chair, raised a hand in farewell before heading out of the door, his scuffed Doc Martens leaving a muddy trail behind him.

With a wry grin, Jared refocused on his paperwork. The sooner he dotted every i, crossed every t, the faster this place could really get off the ground.

* * *

'Any last-minute questions?'

Kristi tore her gaze from the distant view of Sydney's city skyline and turned to Elliott.

'No, I think you've pretty much covered everything.'

Satisfied, Elliott glanced at Jared, who shrugged, grinned.

'A-okay here.'

'Good.' Elliott snapped his clipboard shut. 'Then you're on your own.'

'Thanks, mate.'

As Jared slapped him on the back she waved, quickly dropped her hand when it shook with trepidation as Elliott stepped onto the powerboat and shot away from Lorikeet Island, leaving her alone with the man who intruded her thoughts constantly these days.

She'd been a mess at work the last week, Ros plying her with questions and suggestions for her seven days on the island, and Meg hadn't been much better.

If she didn't want the money for Meg so badly, and couldn't almost taste the promotion Rosanna had dangled in front of her, she would've quit this whole crazy scheme.

But the fact remained: Meg was living in a hovel, with a gorgeous seven-year-old to raise who grew faster than her mum could outfit her, and working her butt off to survive.

Enough money could change all that and she could give her that gift. As for the promotion, a girl could never have too many Louboutin shoes.

Slinging an arm across her shoulder, Jared hugged her close.

'Looks like it's just you and me, kid.'

She stiffened, darted a quick glance around. 'Are there any cameras here?'

His eyes crinkled at the corners when he laughed. 'Safe zone. You weren't listening.'

She shrugged out of his embrace on the pretext of studying some particularly riveting marine life at the water's edge.

'I tuned out when Elliott repeated his spiel for the fifth time.'

'He just wants this to be perfect. It's what he does.'

Feeling bad, she turned back to him. 'I know. He's a great producer. Guess I'm just angsty now we're actually here.'

Squaring his shoulders, he dusted off his hands. 'Right. Let's get cracking.'

Now that the moment of truth had arrived, she didn't want to leave this spot, didn't want to step in front of the cameras to have her every move filmed and scrutinised and analysed.

'First things first. Accommodation.' Jared jerked his thumb east. 'Our humble abodes are that way, apparently.'

'Mmm,' she mumbled, scuffing her sandal in the sand, reluctant to move.

Laying a hand on her shoulder, he squeezed, an innocuous comforting touch that shot a spark of awareness straight through her.

'You can do this.'

Think of the money, think of the promotion.

She'd been thinking of nothing less to keep her motivated—discounting the inordinate amount of time she'd spent thinking about this man and how to approach their enforced proximity over the next week.

She'd replayed every moment of their dinner together, had marvelled at how laid-back he'd been, slipping into comfortable conversation, content to ignore or glide over her silences, her monosyllabic responses.

She'd done her best that night to send him a message: that he could smile and flirt all he liked, she was immune. And while she'd like nothing better than to vent her long-suppressed feelings about how things had ended, harbouring ongoing animosity would make the next seven days unbearable.

So she'd made a decision.

She would be polite but distant.

Respond to his questions but not get too friendly.

Play the part of a woman determined to win the cash while trying to ignore the cameras.

And not, repeat *not*, let Jared and his fabled charm creep under her guard again.

She should've been glad she'd established a cool distance the night at dinner. Instead, a tiny part of her had fallen back under his spell that night and that knowledge was what kept her standing here, her feet riveted to the spot, her heart pounding with fear that the moment she truly embarked on this crazy week would signal the beginning of the end. The end of her peace of mind, the beginning of a possibility. That couldn't last.

'Come on, I'll be with you every step of the way.'

He held out his hand and she stared at it, the broad palm, the long, strong fingers, the curve of his thumb pad.

She didn't want to place her hand in his, to trust him, had learned the hard way it was all an illusion.

Lowering his voice, he said, 'We'll have a ball. It'll be just like old times.'

Old times?

She'd adored him, craved him, loved him so fiercely she could scarcely breathe for wanting him.

He wasn't offering her anything, but for an insane moment, staring into his eyes, so frank, so honest, she wanted to recapture some of that old magic, wanted to feel half as good again.

On a drawn-out sigh, she placed her hand in his, her pulse leaping in recognition as he curled his fingers over hers.

'Okay. Let's do it.'

KRISTI'S BLOG, DAY 1
Lorikeet Island: beautiful views of Sydney, surrounded by the bluest ocean on the planet, perfect weather. I've lasted the first hour without making any major gaffes in front of the cameras. Then again, have sat petrified, sipping soda on the postage-stamp veranda of my 'home' for the next week, watching Jared act all he-man by scoping out the lay of the land.

Don't know why he's bothering. Not like we'll get attacked by any wild animals, right?

Yikes! What was that growling sound?

Oh, only my stomach. Woman does not survive on soda and fresh air alone. Time to rustle up lunch. Baked beans on campfire toast?

I miss Sydney already.

JARED'S BLOG, DAY 1
Not a bad spot. Might take up fishing. Kristi brought too many shoes. She's such a girl.

CHAPTER SIX

Stranded *Survival Tip #6*
Blogging is fun but for ever. Choose your
words wisely.

'YOU ever use Twitter before?'

Kristi shook her head, trying to sneak a peek over Jared's shoulder as he fiddled with his iPhone.

'No time. Work keeps me pretty busy. I email. Facebook page. That's about it.'

His eyes not leaving the screen, he said, 'You don't know what you're missing.'

Her scoffing snort had him darting an amused glance her way.

'What's so special about informing the world what you're up to in one hundred and forty characters or less?'

'It's the challenge, to make your tweet interesting in so few words.'

Typing quickly, he finally laid his phone down, his stare loaded.

'Surely you know how much guys like a challenge?'

'Guys or just you?'

He chuckled. 'Last time I checked I was a guy. Or would you care to verify—?'

'Stop that!' she hissed, jerking her head towards one of the not-so-hidden cameras. 'We're live.'

Dropping his voice to a conspiratorial whisper, he leaned forward and spoke behind his raised hand.

'Viewers love this sort of thing. A bit of light-hearted banter, flirting. Good for ratings.'

He wiggled his eyebrows until the unimpressed twist to her lips relaxed into a smile. 'Sex sells, baby.'

Okay, so he was hamming it up for the cameras. Not that she could blame him. There was something so weirdly unnatural about all of this. As to why anyone would be remotely interested in watching the two of them have dinner or quibble over the last Tim Tam was beyond her.

But she couldn't deny Elliott Barnaby was a genius; and the one salient fact: she was in this for the money, and the promotion.

Faking a huff, she tossed her hair over her shoulder like any screen heroine worth her salt.

'I'm not your baby.'

'You were once.'

He whispered it so softly the cameras wouldn't have a chance of picking it up, her skin prickling with alarm as he scooted closer, his warm breath fanning her neck as he murmured in her ear, 'Want to recreate some of the old magic?'

'No!'

Her body made a mockery of her instant refusal, heat flushing her skin rosy as she inadvertently leaned into him, practically inviting him to slip an arm around her and cradle her close as he used to.

'Liar,' he whispered, his fingertips trailing across the back of her neck and sending a quiver of desire through her as he casually draped an arm over her shoulder, appearing to the whole world as if they were best buddies.

An instant, unexpected, fierce need pounded through her body, setting a relentless tempo, willfully ignoring her supposed immunity to him these days and urging her to be totally reckless, fling herself into his arms, cameras be damned.

But there was a difference between making a fool of herself over this man again and doing it with the general public eagerly looking on, so she slid out from under his arm on the pretext of retrieving his phone.

'Here. Tweet something.'

His low, husky laugh rippled over her, his knowing stare leaving her in little doubt he didn't buy her brush-off for a second.

'Okay. Watch this.'

His thumb flew over the phone's keypad, his grin widening before he handed over the phone.

'Go ahead. Take a look.'

With increasing foreboding she glanced at the screen, her heart skipping a beat, several, as she read his brief message to the cyber world.

Twitter.com/Stranded_Jared
Old flames never die. They just burn brighter
if you fan the fire.

Ignoring the irrational leap of her pulse, and the distinct urge to skip the fanning part and jump directly into the fire, she handed him back the phone.

'You sure you're not a pyromaniac? All this talk of flames and your incessant need to poke at the campfire?'

'Being obtuse won't help.'

He pressed the phone into her palm. 'Your turn.'

'I don't have an account.'

'Elliott set one up for both of us. Yours is under Stranded_Kristi.'

'Of course it is.'

Mustering a sickly sweet smile, she tapped at the phone, saw her PR picture on her Twitter home page.

'Remember, play nice,' he murmured, his wink urging her to do the exact opposite.

She searched her brain for something suitably witty to say, something other than the mundane. In the end, she settled for the partial truth.

Twitter.com/Stranded_Kristi
Ever wish an ex could see you now? Be careful what you wish for!

Jared clutched his chest. 'Harsh.'

'Honest,' she said, handing him back his phone with a smirk. 'I think I'm getting the hang of this Twitter thing.'

He slipped the phone into his pocket with a rueful grin.

'Yeah, just don't go singing my praises too much.'

'No risk of that.'

She stilled as he reached out and touched her cheek, a brief brush of his fingertips that tingled all the way to her toes.

'What happened to the girl who used to look at me with stars in her eyes?'

Not liking this turn of conversation, she shrugged, aimed for levity.

'Stars fade, lose their lustre.'

She knew she'd said the wrong thing the instant he stood, his eyes shuttered, his expression deliberately blank.

'I didn't mean—'

'I know you didn't.'

He turned his back on her, strolled towards the water's edge, staring across the water to the Harbour Bridge glittering like a sparkly coat hanger in the distance.

'You miss it, don't you?'

His shoulders stiffened imperceptibly before he thrust his hands into his pockets, his casual stance at odds with his tense posture.

'Everyone has to retire some time.'

'But that choice was taken away from you by the injury. It's different.'

'I could've come back if I'd wanted to.'

His voice held a wistful edge, a hint of vulnerability she'd never heard from the invincible charmer, and the part of her that had once loved him urged her to go to him, offer what comfort she could.

'Why didn't you? Really?'

She laid a hand on his shoulder, willing him to turn around, to let her comfort him. But he didn't move, continued staring out over the water as if she hadn't spoken.

She wanted to push him for answers, wanted to

use the old philosophy 'a problem shared is a problem halved', but she had no right.

They'd been apart for eight years and she knew little about him beyond what she'd read in the tabloids, knew little beyond what he'd told her when they'd been dating; and that hadn't been much.

No, she had no right to push him for answers, none at all. For answers would give her a glimpse into the guy behind the confident façade, would make it harder for her to pretend they were nothing more than friends.

Despite the bitterness following their break-up, despite the anger that infused every part of her trusting soul until she wanted to wring his neck, after spending a day with him, she was forced to acknowledge the truth.

A small part of her still cared.

Always had, and spending time with him reinforced Meg's theory: maybe she hadn't gone through with her two marriages because of this man and the mark he'd left on her all those years ago.

Call her crazy, call her corny, but she suddenly understood the quaint term 'being spoiled for any other man'. Jared had branded her heart as surely as if he'd taken a heated iron bar and pressed it there, leaving her burned, marked as his.

Her hand fell from his shoulder and she stepped

away, surprised when he turned to face her, his expression inscrutable in the shadows.

'Ever had someone have a profound effect on your life?'

Whatever she'd been expecting, it wasn't that and she cautiously nodded, not wanting to turn this into a conversation about her.

'My folks, I guess. They were amazing.'

'You would've done anything for them, right?'

'Uh-huh.'

She had no idea where he was going with this, assuming he was indebted to a mentor, maybe a coach, which had influenced his decision to retire.

Dragging a hand through his hair, he shook his head. 'Getting injured, going through rehab, seeing all those injured and partially disabled kids gave me time to think about where my life was heading. Through all those boring hydrotherapy sessions I figured it was time to do something else than hit a ball around a court.'

'Something you were darn good at, mind you.'

'I was, wasn't I?'

His proud grin warmed her heart. 'Now that's the modest Jared Malone I know and love.'

Yikes! She'd spoken too quickly, made a gaffe of monumental proportions.

To his credit, his smile didn't slip but she saw caution creep into his eyes.

'Glad to hear I haven't lost any of my multitudes of adoring fans.'

She could've left it there, should've left it there, but she'd never taken the safe option when it came to this man.

'Is that all I ever was to you?'

'You know better than that.'

Did she?

They'd had a whirlwind romance that lasted six months. He'd moved to Sydney, they'd met at a PR event; she'd been smitten the first time he'd smiled at her. And while he'd lavished her with compliments, spent every spare moment off the courts with her, she knew she'd fallen harder.

He'd never said he'd loved her, never made any promises, and watching him walk away had broken her heart. Her gullible, impressionable heart that used to leap into the palm of his hand every time he was near.

Thank goodness she'd grown up, wised up, toughened up.

'It's late. Think I'll turn in.'

She hadn't taken two steps before his hand slid around her waist and she stopped, held her breath, aware of the inky darkness, the soft lapping of waves on the shore and the heat, so much heat, from his simple touch.

'We were good together.'

What the heck did that mean? They could be again? Not bloody likely!

She spun around, expecting to brush off his hand. It didn't move and she found herself tantalisingly close to a body she'd once known intimately, a body giving off signals she didn't have a hope of ignoring.

'What do you want from me, Jared?'

She watched a million responses flicker across his face, before his mouth quirked into that familiar, sexy, heart-rending smile.

Tugging her close, he gazed into her eyes and she knew right that very second, she was in trouble. Big Trouble.

'What do I want?'

His gaze dropped to her lips as anticipation fizzed through her like expensive champagne.

'This.'

His kiss catapulted her back to a time filled with special memories and the sweetness of first love, a time where a charming, gregarious and utterly devastating man had swept her off her feet. A time she'd lost all sense of reason until it was too late.

Which begged the question: what on earth was she doing letting him kiss her now?

CHAPTER SEVEN

Stranded *Survival Tip #7*
Avoid board games to pass time. Arguments assured.

KRISTI'S BLOG, DAY 2
One down, six to go. Honestly, how long can one week drag?

As fellow 'strandees' can't read each other's blogs I'm going to be blunt.

Being stuck on this island is KILLING me!

No Italian milk hot chocolates from Max Brenner, no Caesar salads from my favourite café in Bondi, no lunchtime retail therapy dashes to check out shoes.

Worst of all? No peace of mind.

Word of advice to anyone contemplating a similar madness? Don't do it.

Being cooped up with an ex is similar to getting a bikini wax: pure torture.

Wouldn't be so bad if I didn't like him but

*we're talking about THE Jared Malone.
Ladies, you know what I mean. You've seen
him with his shirt off courtside a thousand
times, you've seen him interviewed and heard
his snappy one liners, and you've seen that
killer smile.*

Say no more.

I'm a wreck.

*Pretending like everything is just oh-so-
casual is tough. Staying immune to the damn
charmer tougher.*

*See, this is the problem with no TV. You're
forced to read or talk and there are only so
many back issues of Vogue I can skim. Which
leaves me back at square one: talking to the
guy, laughing at his jokes, acting all matey
when…when…heck, I'm not supposed to like
him any more!*

Repeat after me: six days to go…

*JARED'S BLOG, DAY 2
Hanging out with Kristi is cool. Like being
with an old buddy and not having to make an
effort. Next six days going to be a blast.*

She was killing him.

With every squirt of the suntan lotion tube,
every slow, deliberate rub down her arm, down her

long legs, with every wriggle of her cute butt as she got comfortable on her beach towel, she was killing him.

So much for a week of banter, flirtation, nothing too heavy.

As Kristi rolled from her back to her front, inadvertently squeezing her breasts together, spilling over the top of the tiniest green bikini he'd ever seen, Jared bit back a groan and resumed the mundane task of gathering kindle.

This was all his fault.

He'd never meant to kiss her, had intended on having a little fun while on the island, had wanted to keep things light-hearted.

Then she'd gone all serious on him, probing into his reasons behind quitting the tennis world, had opened a chasm in his heart he ignored every day, and he'd lost it.

Kissing her had been the lesser of two evils, for he had no intention of delving into his psyche and the constant reminder he would never play tennis again.

His manager and coach had pushed him to see a psychologist after the injury, mandatory for any pro cut down in his prime.

He'd faced the usual questions: how do you feel about your injury? Are you resentful? Angry? Liable to go off the deep end?

Okay, so that last one hadn't been phrased quite like that, but the uptight geek in his fancy glass-enclosed office that hadn't spent a day on a court in his life had prodded and probed his mind until he would've said anything to get out of there.

The thing was no amount of therapy sessions with an elite sports psychologist would ease the ache of losing a part of himself, the only part of him linking him to his flaky parents.

And that was what peed him off the most.

The fact he cared.

After living through the nightmare of their dys-functional relationship, after surviving their total oblivion to having a son, the second he'd been dis-covered and won Junior Wimbledon his parents had done an about-face.

He'd initially hated their sudden fawning, had doubted every overture they'd made, until the locked away part of him that had always craved their approval cracked and let them in.

The smart, cynical side of him knew why they'd done it. To bask in the reflected glory of his triumphs, to share in his fame.

Yet the vulnerable little boy desperate for a smidgeon of affection from his parents thrived under their long-overdue attention, enjoyed having them courtside, applauding him, fist-pumping along every hard-fought victory, sharing in his Grand Slam titles.

So what would happen to their tentative relationship now he'd quit? Considering the sparse visits during his rehab, the lack of phone calls recently, he knew. Whoever had coined the phrase *the truth hurt* had a courtside seat to his life.

Now this.

Kristi made an impolite slurping as she guzzled her favourite soda and he raised his head, watching her.

He didn't give a damn what the cameras picked up, didn't care if they captured an image of a schmuck blinded by the only woman to ever get remotely close to him.

He'd flirted with the world's most beautiful women, from film stars to royalty, and contrary to paparazzi reports hadn't slept with them all. He hadn't had the time, focused solely on being the best and obtaining the number-one ranking.

Tennis had consumed his life for so long. Now it was gone. And while his priorities had shifted into the business arena, a small part of him was terrified he'd revert back to that lost kid who wasn't good enough unless he held a racket.

Kristi knew nothing of his past and he'd like to keep it that way. She might be the closest thing he'd ever had to a relationship but that didn't mean he'd lose his head again.

As for his heart, he'd locked that away a long

time ago, safe from trust and inevitable pain when people you loved didn't give a toss either way.

'Done with the caveman routine?'

The organ he refused to acknowledge lurched as he glanced up, saw Kristi on her side, propped on an elbow, wearing that sinful green bikini and a reluctant smile.

She'd been frosty towards him over dinner, with more of the same since they'd arrived on the island, but under his constant barrage of teasing she was finally starting to thaw.

Not that he blamed her. From her angry outburst when he'd picked her up the other night, she hadn't forgiven him for choosing his tennis career over her all those years ago.

But he'd had no choice.

Not that he'd go delving into his reasons why now.

For their time on the island he wanted to recapture some of their old magic, wanted to make her laugh and fire back those scathing one-liners as she used to, wanted to see her eyes sparkle just for him, for old times' sake.

Hands on hips, he wrenched his straying gaze away from the tempting expanses of flesh on display. 'Weren't you the one who wanted to toast marshmallows tonight?'

'Did *I* say that?'

She pressed a hand to her chest and his gaze followed, shooting down his intentions to keep his distance.

'Do you even have any?'

She chuckled, lowered her sunglasses to stare at him over the top. 'Maybe you should've asked that before planning to build a bonfire that can be seen in New Zealand.'

Adding another branch onto the growing pile, he feigned indifference.

'I'm surprised you could fit any marshmallows in your case, what with that mobile shoe shop you carry around.'

Her eyes narrowed, the corners of her mouth twitching. 'Are you dissing my shoes?'

'Merely making an observation.'

With a little huff that was so adorable he wanted to kiss her senseless, she pouted.

'I'll have you know it takes effort to look this good.'

His gaze raked her from top to toe, lingering on her curves, the hollow of her hip, the dip of her collarbone, remembering how he'd traced every inch of her once, how he hadn't been able to get enough.

Logically, he knew it would be foolish to resurrect the past, when nothing fundamental had changed. Kristi was a relationship type of girl. He was a guy who had no intention of getting emotionally involved with anyone.

Physically, his body was on memory overload, sifting through every incredible, erotic encounter the two of them had ever had.

'You're not looking at my shoes.'

Dragging his gaze to meet hers, he raised an eyebrow. 'You're not wearing any.'

She scooped up a spangly flip-flop, dangling it from a finger.

'What's this?'

'Suitcase filler?'

'Heathen,' she muttered, sliding her sunglasses back into place and rolling onto her back. 'Get back to your wood gathering. It's what you Neanderthals are good at.'

'Sticks and stones,' he said, much more at ease with this banter than last night's emotion-charged discussion.

Pointing at the diminutive wood pile, she smirked. 'More sticks. Less stones.'

Dusting off his hands, he planted them squarely on his hips, glared her down.

'If someone spent less time criticising and more time helping, we might actually get this fire built before dusk.'

'And ruin your he-man reputation? Not likely.'

With a shooing wiggle of her fingers in a dismissive wave, she rolled over onto her tummy and turned her head the other way, leaving him with an ideal view of her great butt.

He'd like nothing better than to march over there, grab her and pick up where they left off last night. Instead, he clenched his hands several times, shook them out before turning on his heel and heading off in search for more wood.

His sole intention for being stuck on this island for a week might revolve around priceless free publicity for the rec centre, but the more time he spent sparring with Kristi, the further his intentions would evolve.

Into something he couldn't contemplate.

Grateful he'd dropped out of a camera's vision, he roundly cursed as he picked up a piece of wood and hurled it as far as he could.

Twitter.com/Stranded_Jared
Playing best buddies with an ex sucks.

Twitter.com/Stranded_Kristi
Cosy campfire, toasted marshmallows, hot guy. What? A girl can look, right?

'Don't go getting any ideas.'

'Huh?' Kristi stretched, rubbed her tummy and moaned as Jared popped a marshmallow off the end of the stick, juggling it between hands and blowing on it.

'We are *not* doing this every night.'

'Considering I've just consumed half a bag of marshmallows and can barely move, you won't get any complaints from me.'

Throwing the marshmallow in the air, he tilted his head back, caught it in his open mouth first try.

'That's what you say now but I bet you'll be back to your bossy best tomorrow, making me gather firewood while you loll around.'

Shaking her head as he offered her the last marshmallow, she said, 'Think of the ratings. All those women viewers out there will be glued to their screens, starry-eyed over your flexing muscles as you gather wood.'

Flicking his glance over her denim cargo shorts and white ribbed singlet top, he raised an eyebrow.

'I think you're doing more than your fair share for ratings, what with that scrap of material passing as a bikini you wore today.'

He'd noticed! She'd been furious after that kiss, angrier with herself than him. She'd expect something like that from him considering his blasé attitude, as if they could pick up their relationship and run with it.

But her responding to the kiss…now that was another matter. Oh, she'd been resistant at first.

But the longer his lips had coaxed her, plied her with a skill that still left her breathless after all this time, she'd lost her mind, forgetting every sane reason why she shouldn't respond.

She didn't know what was worse: her mortification that she'd kissed him back or the discovery her resilience against this man was under serious threat now she'd let him in a fraction.

Like any woman scorned, she'd mulled over payback. And deliberately worn the most provocative bikini she owned today. Foolish, maybe, but she wanted to rattle him as much as he'd rattled her last night with that unexpected kiss. What she hadn't banked on was the heat of awareness prickling her body every time he glanced her way.

She'd moved on eight years ago, had two diamond solitaires to prove it, but when Jared looked at her in that special way he catapulted her right back to a time when she'd once been crazy for him.

'It's supposed to be realistic. What else is a girl supposed to wear on an island?'

She only just caught his muttered 'a neck-to-knee bathing suit'.

Oh, yeah, she was getting to him.

She should feel vindicated. Instead, a strange sense of deflation crept over her. What was she doing? Playing some silly tit-for-tat game when she'd vowed to keep her distance.

Her response to his kiss had been an aberration, a reaction of a woman who hadn't had a date let alone a peck of a kiss in ages. Best she ignored it, reverted to her original plan: ignore, ignore, ignore.

Hugging her knees to her chest, she folded her arms, rested her chin on them, watching the shadows from the fire play across his face, highlighting a cheekbone here, a jaw line there.

He'd always been handsome but there was something about him now…an assuredness he'd never had when they'd first met.

Winning a few Grand Slams did that for a guy, but there was more to it. From all reports, and if she believed everything she read, he'd had a cushy life, the Aussie darling of the tennis circuit, the golden boy who couldn't put a volley wrong.

Yet there was a new hardened edge to him, as if life had smashed more than a few aces his way.

'You're staring.'

'At the fire.'

He prodded the fire with a long stick. 'Nope, at me.'

She should leave things alone but the atmosphere, the silence, was conducive to chatting. It was okay to freeze him out emotionally but surely she could make small talk?

Curiosity egged her on; she was dying to ask if

all the rumours were true, if he'd done half the things the magazines said he had.

'Can't get enough of me, huh?'

He leaned back on outstretched elbows, the sky-blue cotton T-shirt pulled taut across his muscular chest. For someone who'd been out of the game a year, he hadn't lost his physique. Then again, twelve months of intensive rehab would've kept him fit.

'Your ego hasn't changed a bit.'

She rolled her eyes, bit back the urge to laugh along with him.

'You've changed.'

Despite his light tone, she could sense a serious undercurrent and, while she didn't want to get into a deep and meaningful rehashing their past, he'd piqued her curiosity. How did he see her now?

Playing it cool, she wound a strand of hair around her finger, checked for split ends.

''Course I've changed. New hairstyle, new wardrobe—'

'New attitude.'

'What did you expect? For me to be the same naïve, starry-eyed girl you…hung out with?'

She'd almost said loved but that wasn't true. Jared had never loved her. Despite all the attention, all the good times, all the intimate moments they'd shared, he hadn't loved her. Not enough to stick around.

His eyes narrowed, as if he could see right through her.

'You've got a streetwise edge these days.'

'You don't like it?'

He glanced away, his answer right there before he spoke.

'I liked my old Krissie.'

She bit her tongue to stop blurting she was never *his* to begin with.

Uneasy with this turn of conversation, she needed a diversion.

'Tell me about Florida.'

His shoulders tensed, an instant giveaway he didn't want to talk about it.

'How was it when you first left Sydney and settled there?'

He sat up, dusted his hands off, resumed poking at the fire, staring into the flames.

'Not much to tell. I trained like the devil, hung out with other up-and-comers, did everything my coach and manager told me to, that's it.'

He'd told her virtually nothing. She could leave it at that but, knowing Jared, he'd swing the interrogation right back on her and there was no way she'd dwell on a time they'd been crazy for each other.

'You rocketed into the top one hundred in your first year. Must've been some ride.'

'Pretty boring, actually. Early mornings,

rigorous training schedule, strict diet, limited down time.'

He continued to stare into the fire, his face devoid of emotion, which only fuelled her curiosity.

'So all those blondes came later?'

He finally glanced her way, a flicker of a smile tugging his lips.

'Don't forget the brunettes and the redheads.'

'And the princesses, the movie starlets, the supermodels.'

She ticked them off on her fingers, could've easily covered both hands and feet with the reports of playboy Jared and his conquests.

'Yeah, those too.'

He smiled, instantly alleviating the reservations of moments ago.

'Anyone serious among your harem?'

'Hell, no!'

His vehement response startled her but before she could respond, he rushed on. 'Not the relationship type. You know that.'

As if she needed reminding. The day he'd walked in on her in her room-mate's wedding dress was embedded in her memory, an annoying spur that niggled despite the years gone by. His shocked expression, horrified and shuttered when she'd made that half-serious comment about it being their turn soon.

When he'd initially left for Florida she'd spent many wasted hours replaying that moment, wondering if things would've been different if she hadn't said it, if she'd passed it off as a flyaway comment.

Instead, her highly strung emotions had snowballed from that moment. He'd pulled away, she'd pushed for answers he didn't want to give. So, yeah, she knew he wasn't the relationship type, yet hearing him articulate it now after so much time had elapsed still had the power to hurt.

'Hey, if anyone knows what you're like, it's me.'

She inwardly cringed as the words left her mouth, her proclamation sounding too personal, too close for comfort.

He stood, threw his stick on the fire, took a few steps towards the wood pile before turning back to face her.

'Don't go getting any ideas.'

'Like?'

'Like taking our time here as meaning anything more than what it is.'

'And what's that?'

'Two old friends getting reacquainted.'

'Bull.'

She leaped to her feet, marched towards him until she stood two feet away, in his face.

'I bought that trite old line eight years ago but not any more.'

'What line—?'

'The one about you not being the settling type. About not wanting to get involved.'

She gestured towards Sydney's skyline glittering in the distance.

'You wouldn't be back here if you didn't want to settle. You wouldn't be stuck on this island with me if you weren't already involved.'

He swiped a hand over his clenched jaw. 'You don't know what you're talking about—'

'Elliott told me you're doing this because you're backing some youth centre in Kings Cross? If that isn't involvement, I don't know what is! You could've just thrown a zillion dollars their way but, uh-uh, you're here, being filmed for some crazy documentary, to gain some high-priced advertising slots.'

She jabbed him in the chest, twice, for good measure. 'That's involvement! And it's great. So don't spin me some bull about you not getting involved because you do.'

Just not with me.

A realisation she'd come to terms with eight years earlier, yet reinforcing the knowledge didn't make it any easier.

He held up his hands, backed away. 'Look, after what happened last night, I just don't want any confusion.'

Clenching her hands, she deliberately released them before she slugged him.

'I'm not confused. *You* kissed *me*; it's what guys like you do.'

A frown settled between those startling hazel eyes. 'Guys like me?'

'You need me to spell it out?'

'Please do.'

'You're a player. A little charm here, a little flirting there, the odd heated glance, throw in a kiss or two, you like to have women adore you.'

His frown deepened, the groove slashing between his brows not detracting from his good looks one iota.

'Harsh.'

'But true.'

Shaking his head, he said, 'You don't know me at all.'

The realisation slammed into her and she staggered a few steps back, stopping short of slapping her head.

She'd never known him.

Not the real Jared Malone; behind the driven ambition, behind the sexy smiles and laid-back attitude, behind the charming exterior.

He'd only ever let her see what he wanted her to see, holding her at bay emotionally during the time they dated. She'd been so busy nursing a broken heart back then, she hadn't seen the truth.

That she'd never really known this man at all.

Quelling the urge to rub at the ache nestling in her chest, she shrugged.

'You're right, I guess I don't.'

The prickle of tears took her completely by surprise and she blinked, damned if she'd let him see her cry over him. Spinning around, she dashed towards her hut.

'Kristi, wait.'

She didn't.

She was through waiting for anything associated with Jared Malone.

CHAPTER EIGHT

Stranded *Survival Tip #8*
Real men erect tents.

KRISTI'S BLOG, DAY 3
Been the epitome of a polite island companion all day.

Haven't talked much beyond, 'How are you?' and, 'Nice cup of billy tea.'

Safer this way. Last night's chat? Not good. All the signs of an irrational woman cooped up on an island with a sexy ex too long.

Kinda like that syndrome victims acquire with their kidnappers, when the proximity gives them the delusion of falling in love?

Yeah, that's exactly it! I'm a woman, he's the only other guy on the island, stands to reason I want to get up close and personal, right? Want to delve into his psyche? Get to know him better?

Problem is, have tried this before, eight

*years ago to be precise. Didn't work then,
what makes me think it'll work now?*

*He's closed up tight. Even got all snotty
when I mentioned his backing the youth centre. Touchy, touchy, touchy.*

*With only four days to survive, must stick
with plan.*
Avoid at all costs.

JARED'S BLOG, DAY 3
*Have never built a campfire before. Not a
bad job. Kept the bugs away.*

*What is it with women and fires? They
want to get all cosy and chatty? Annoying.*

Have disassembled wood pile today.

'Stupid challenge, stupid island, stupid man,'
Kristi muttered, fiddling with a tent peg for the
tenth time and watching the front collapse again.

'Need some help?'

She glared at Jared's perfectly erected two-man
tent, pegs spaced equally, ropes taut, royal-blue
tarpaulin gaily silhouetting the sun, and bit back
her first retort of where he could stick his help.

While concentrating on keeping her distance
from him was now a full-time job, she hadn't lost
sight of the prize. She needed to win that prize
money so proving herself at these challenges was

essential. Either that or make such a huge fool of herself people would take pity on her and vote for her anyway.

'No, thanks.'

She ducked her head, concentrated on driving the peg into the ground, only to have the darn thing slip from her fingers and the entire side wall collapse.

She let fly a string of pithy curses under her breath and blinked back the sudden sting of tears, which had little to do with the tent and everything to do with the man offering his assistance.

Yeah, as if he cared. He'd been distantly polite all day, responding to her remoteness with much the same and she'd been glad. If they stayed aloof she could pretend their little heart-to-heart last night had never happened.

After his revelation, should be easy.

'Don't go getting any ideas. Like taking our time here as meaning anything more than what it is.'

Foolishly, that was exactly what she'd done, despite her determination to keep her distance. All the logic in the world hadn't stopped her from reading more into his charm, his flirting, his kiss.

Damn it! The guy had *kissed* her and he expected her not to go getting any ideas?

She was glad she'd blurted the truth about why he was here, despite Elliott mentioning it was a touchy subject and to not let on she knew. What he was doing was admirable, so why the secrecy?

She knew. Just another way for him to maintain his distance, to keep her out of his life. Fine with her.

She stood, gave the peg a childish kick and marched towards the water's edge, grateful the cameras had whirred off a few minutes ago.

If footage of the camping challenge Elliott had set them was interesting, it would've won an Emmy with her petulant outburst. Viewers lapped up all that reality-throw-a-barney rubbish.

'Let me help.'

He laid a hand on her arm and she stiffened, hating how his touch could make her crave him, hating how much she wanted to give in to him more.

Where was her pride? Where was her plan to stay aloof? A bit hard when all she wanted to do was turn around, fling herself into his arms and sob her little bruised heart out.

'Better not.'

She shrugged off his hand, not daring to look at him. 'I might go getting *ideas*.'

'I knew you were still peed off about that.'

'Kudos to you!'

Blowing out an exasperated breath, she folded her arms, little protection against a guy of his calibre.

'I'm just being honest with you.'

'Bull!'

She swung to face him, her plan to stay cool blowing sky-high in the face of his nonchalant self-denial.

Jabbing a finger in his direction, she said, 'You're not being honest with yourself so how the heck can you be honest with me?'

He didn't say a word, merely looked at her with a patient expression, patronising beyond belief.

'Tell me this. What did you think happened between us eight years ago?'

Wariness crept into his eyes, turning them intriguing caramel.

'We had fun.'

'Fun. That's it? Nothing more?'

He shifted slightly, his feet shuffling in the sand. 'I was only ever going to be in Sydney for a short time. You knew the score.'

She thought she had. But in her romantic dreams their score had been love-all instead of deuce, a tie of crazy emotions and cool aloofness when he left.

'So you're telling me there were no emotions involved?'

Another direct hit when his gaze slid away and focused on the shrubbery fringing the beach.

'We had a great six months, Krissie. It had to end eventually. Why dredge up the past now?'

Her eyes narrowed as she took a step towards

him, enjoying the flicker of alarm as his gaze re-focused on her.

'Because you're a fool if you think for one second that what happened between us in the past isn't affecting us right now.'

His jaw clenched, clamping down on a host of truths she needed to hear; or was that just wishful thinking on her part?

'Aren't you the least bit curious why I'm so peed off at you? The real reason?'

His lips compressed in an unimpressed line, guilt shifting like furtive shadows darting across his face.

'I know you blame me for how things ended—'

'You think?'

She calmed her loud voice with effort, rolled her shoulders to work out some of the tension, all too aware that once she started down this track she'd have to finish it.

In a way, venting might alleviate some of her residual anger, a bitterness that ran so deep she hadn't known it existed until he'd strutted back into her life pretending he'd never been away.

'You knew our dating had a time limit.'

Defensive to the end. Well, she had a few truths for him.

'Yeah, but what I didn't know was that once you reached that time limit you'd cut and run without even seeing me for a proper goodbye.'

'I don't like farewells.'

Unclenching her fist long enough to jab him in the chest, she stepped closer, invaded his personal space, righteous indignation spurring her to make her point, to make the most of this opportunity after all these years.

'That's lame, even by your standards.'

When he didn't venture any further denials, she exhaled on a long, low whistle and pivoted away, taking several steps before swinging to face him again.

'You took one look at me in that wedding dress and had a coronary. You didn't give me a chance to tell you I was joking about us doing it for real, you didn't give me a chance to do much of anything after that.'

Swallowing an unexpected sob bubbling in the back of her throat, she pinned him with an accusatory stare.

'Throwing that ultimatum at you was stupid. But I was hurting. I hadn't seen you. Then you just hopped on that plane and left, just like that, and I'll never forgive you for robbing me of a real chance at closure.'

He opened his mouth, closed it again, shook his head.

What could he say? She'd said enough for both

of them, encapsulating their break-up in a few harsh sentences.

Strangely, she felt better, the offloading of her latent resentment cathartic. But she hadn't finished. She'd had her say about their past; time to get the present sorted.

'And you're wrong. Dead wrong. There were emotions involved before so tell me, what's zapping between us now?'

'Sexual attraction.'

It was her turn to flinch as he leaned forward, so close she could smell his crisp, clean cologne, could feel the heat radiating off him.

'As *I* recall, we had that in spades. Good to see some things never change.'

Back on safe turf for him, flirting, using his sexuality as a weapon to avoid anything remotely deep and meaningful. While she might have responded in like eight years ago, what he'd said last night had snatched the sarong from over her eyes.

She'd loved him eight years ago, really loved him in the way a woman pictured herself walking up the aisle in a stunning white dress, having kids with him, growing old with him.

She'd lied to him. That flyaway comment about them getting married in the future? She'd meant every word of it. But what was the point of telling him now? It would undermine her whole argument that he'd robbed her of closure by leaving without giving her a chance.

He'd been her first love, the kind of love a girl never forgot and, while she might have kidded herself into believing those feelings were long dead, it had taken a mere three days in his company to peel away the layers and reveal the truth.

He still had the power to shake her to her very foundations.

Him, a guy who couldn't commit, who didn't do emotions, who had the audacity to tell her, *'Don't go getting any ideas.'*

The bloody cheek of the man!

Stifling the urge to bop him on the nose, she lowered her tone to silky smooth.

'So what you're saying is you want me for my body?'

His intense gaze slid down her body, bold, provocative, setting her alight and almost ruining her determination to take a stance.

But this was too important and no way in hell would she let him get away with it again. Eight years was a long time to wise up and now she'd finally had her say she had no intention of succumbing to his fall-back, fail-safe charm.

When he met her eyes again, his wicked grin sent a shot of pure lust licking along her pebbled skin, leaving her resolve shaky.

'Yeah, I want you.'

Hoping he couldn't see her shift slightly thanks to the sudden wobble in her knees, she took hold of his hand.

'Here's a tip.'

She placed his hand on her hip. 'If you want this.'

She raised his hand and placed it directly over her heart, desperately trying to ignore how it pounded at the touch of his hand near her breast. 'You first have to go through this.'

Surprise parted his lips before he clamped them shut and snatched his hand. With a shake of his head, eyes wild, he took a step back, drew in a breath, several.

She'd never seen him so rattled and the fact he'd reacted like this confirmed what she already knew.

No matter how aloof or cool he liked to pretend to be, something more than attraction simmered beneath his cool exterior.

When she'd given up hope he'd answer, he finally said, 'I don't want to hurt you. Don't you get that?'

Squaring her shoulders, she went for broke.

'A little late for that, don't you think?'

The horror crinkling his face almost made her laugh.

'Are you saying you're in love with me again?'

'Hell, no!'

Her vehement refusal had his mouth twitching.

'I meant you've already done that. I think I can survive anything you throw my way these days.'

'Even if all I want is a fling?'

She'd never settle for anything remotely like a fling but for a tiny, infinitesimal second, she almost wished she would.

'You're a smart guy, you figure it out.'

She touched his chest directly over his heart, lightly, a brush of her fingertips that jump-started her own and had him leaping back as if she'd electrocuted him.

He turned on his heel and strode away as fast as his long, athletic legs could carry him.

She should've been sad, hurt. Instead, a satisfying vindication had her smiling as she noted every rigid, resistant line of his body.

Jared could verbally deny any hint of emotion between them but he couldn't hide his body language.

She'd seen the same tension in his shoulders, his hands, his face, every time he walked out on the court. He'd given his all to tennis, had played like a man possessed, as if he had something to prove each and every game.

It was what had made him the best, had propelled him to the number-one world ranking and kept him there for years.

He reserved that tension for what he cared about,

what he was passionate about and, right now, despite all his protestations, he still cared about her.

The scary thing was, did she really want him to do anything about it?

Jared stomped back to his hut, his bung knee getting a thorough workout while he all but ran across the sand. Away from Kristi and her damn home truths.

It wasn't enough she'd kept him up most of last night, her accusation that he was emotionally invested in Activate resonating for hours.

Uh-uh, now she had to go and rehash the past with her own scathing brand of honesty.

It stung. All of it.

Until now, he'd explained away his actions during their break-up—if only to himself—as justified.

She'd taken a light-hearted fling and read more into it. She'd started to cling and make demands he'd had no hopes or intentions of fulfilling. She'd made that outlandish ultimatum, asking him to choose between her and his career. All her fault.

Or so he'd told himself all this time.

When the reality was something entirely different.

Maybe he'd been young and stupid and driven to succeed at the only thing he was truly good at, the only thing that had ever garnered attention from his folks, but he could've handled their break-up differently.

All the self-justification, all the excuses in the world, couldn't change the fact he'd been scared, terrified in fact, of how she'd made him feel in such a short space of time.

Being with Kristi had been easy, comfortable, yet filled with a constant buzz that he'd only ever emulated by winning his first Grand Slam title.

She'd made him feel good about himself, as if he could achieve anything. And how had he repaid her? By walking out on her without a backward glance.

When she'd made that demand on the phone during their last phone call he'd given her a quick brush-off, mumbling his obligations to his fledgling career, bade her a trite 'all the best' and hung up.

She'd deserved better.

And now, discovering how much she'd invested in them back then opened up an old wound thought healed. At best, he owed her an apology.

Swiping a weary hand across his face, he turned back, hoping she'd hear him out.

When he reached the beach, she'd vanished. Following her footprints in the sand, he picked up the pace, finally catching her near a rocky outcrop overlooking Sydney city in the distance.

'Krissie?'

She turned, her mutinous expression at odds with the tracks of dried tears running in parallel lines down her cheeks, and something inside him broke.

Even when he'd dumped her on the phone, she hadn't cried. Called him a few choice names, but not a hint of a sob in sight. She'd let him off the hook easily, too easily. Time to make amends.

Wrapping her arms around her middle—to ward off the cold or him, he wasn't sure—she thrust her chin up in defiance.

'Figured it out already, huh?'

'You said I was a smart guy. Why do I feel so dumb?'

She didn't budge an inch, remote, unobtainable, as he silently called himself every kind of fool for hurting this special woman.

'You tell me.'

He took a step forward, held out a hand, which she ignored.

'I owe you an apology.'

'For?'

Damn, she was magnificent. From the top of her wind-tousled wild hair to the bottom of her inappropriately designer-clad feet, every inch of her screamed pride.

She wouldn't let him off easy this time. Uh-uh, this time she'd make him grovel.

'For being a coward. For being dense. For treating you appallingly when we broke up.'

Her mouth softened a fraction and he pushed the advantage.

'I could use the excuse I was young and stupid but the truth is, no matter how brilliant we were together back then, I would've run from commitment. It just wasn't the right time.'

Understanding shone from her eyes, blazing with a jumble of emotions he had no hope of deciphering.

'You weren't the only one who was young and stupid.'

Her arms fell to her sides, her shoulders relaxed and loose. 'That horribly cringe-worthy ultimatum I gave you was just plain wrong. I put you in an impossible position.'

'Yeah, you did.'

He tempered his comment with a soft smile, buoyed when she smiled right back.

'I'm sorry, Krissie. Forgive me?'

This time, he wouldn't offer her his hand in the hope she'd take it. Instead, he snagged her hand, held on tight despite her slight tug of resistance.

'I'll think about it.'

His smile widened. 'Good. While you're thinking about it, want to take a walk?'

* * *

Kristi fell into step beside Jared, little rockets of sensation shooting up her arm and into orbit the harder he squeezed her hand.

They shouldn't be doing this, strolling along a moonlit beach, hand in hand. It reeked of romance and she'd given up on that with this man a long time ago.

His apology had softened her, had gone some way to assuaging the resentment lodged in her heart, but she couldn't throw away all her reservations at once.

Jared wanted a fling.

He'd virtually said as much with all that talk of sexual attraction and possible flings. All very cut and dried and easy for him; flirt a little, get physical, walk away at the end. As if she'd ever agree to that! Once was enough.

'I've been thinking about what you said.'

His low tone shattered the companionable silence, shattered the illusion that for a moment they were two people in perfect sync taking a lovely stroll along a deserted stretch of sand.

'Yeah?'

He stopped, leaving her no option but to do the same, giving her opportunity to slide her hand out from his, and she took it.

'About me being invested in the rec centre.'

'And?'

'You're right.'

He shook his head, his tortured expression revealing he was none too pleased with the admission. 'It was about the money at first, giving something back. But seeing all those partially disabled kids in rehab, then the street kids around the Cross when I was scoping sites, really got to me.'

'That's nothing to be ashamed of.'

She touched his arm, trying to convey her admiration, her respect. Many sporting stars financially supported kids' foundations but not many took the time to attend personally, let alone spend a week on a deserted island for publicity.

Pain contorted his features before he carefully blanked them, forced a smile.

'We're just full of confessions tonight.'

It was her turn to feel uncomfortable. He might have unburdened himself, but she still had a few secrets up her sleeve, secrets she had no intention of confessing.

'I'm glad you can talk to me.'

She held her breath as he reached out, his fingertips grazing her cheek in the softest caress. 'I always could.'

But you still left anyway.

It would always come back to that. No matter what he said now, or how far she was willing to forgive him, she could never forget the fact he'd left her.

Battling a surge of heat to her cheeks, she shrugged and turned away on the pretext of staring at the view of Sydney in the distance.

'I guess some things don't change.'

He touched her shoulder and she clamped down on the urge to lean into him. 'We've both changed. Maybe the real question is have we changed enough to move on from the past?'

He used the royal 'we' when he meant her. Had she changed enough to move on from the past, from what they'd shared, from what they'd lost?

Taking a deep breath, she met his curious gaze head-on. 'Honestly? I don't know.'

'Okay, then.'

She had no idea if he'd agreed with what she said, if he was okaying her right to be honest or her right to indecision.

What she did know was the longer they stood here, almost toe to toe, tension crackling between them, the harder it was for her to not say 'screw the past' and jump feet first into the present.

His gaze slid to her lips, lingered, and she inhaled sharply, her lips tingling with expectation.

'Have you figured out what you want?' she blurted, her insides trembling along with her resolve as he leaned towards her, inch by exquisitely torturous inch, lowering his head, the heat radiating off him scorching.

Her eyelids fluttered shut, her head tilting ever so slightly to receive his kiss.

When he rested his forehead against hers and murmured, 'Damned if I know,' she couldn't agree more.

Twitter.com/Stranded_Jared
Get me out of here.

Twitter.com/Stranded_Kristi
Have really started to dig this place. Purely for the scenery, of course.

CHAPTER NINE

Stranded *Survival Tip #9*
Want to humiliate him on camera? Ask him to hold your purse.

KRISTI'S BLOG, DAYS 4–5
Elliott will be lapping this up. Jared has ensured we spend every waking hour in front of the cameras the last two days. An avoidance technique, obviously. Doesn't want a repeat of our little confrontational conversation during the camping challenge. Might start calling him Ostrich Boy...burying his head in the sand and all that.

What he doesn't understand is that he can't avoid me for ever. And the cameras are on timers so if I plan my ambush just right...he doesn't stand a chance.

That, or hog-tie him and drag him to the camera-safe locations on the island.

Of course, I'd get the whole tying-up thing

*on camera first. Wouldn't that make for inter-
esting TV? Would definitely score points in
the prize-winning stakes.*

*He may have the muscles to erect a tent bet-
ter than me but I definitely nailed the swimming challenge. And I caught five fish to his
measly two in the fishing challenge.*

I rock!

Show me the money!

JARED'S BLOG, DAYS 4-5

Only two days to go.

*I've made it through Wimbledon semi-
finals with back spasms.*

*I survived a five-set marathon to win the
US Open, twice.*

I can do this!

*(By the way, aren't girls supposed to be
squeamish about baiting hooks with live bait?
Can't believe she out-fished me! I'd rather
lose the hundred grand than let the boys dis-
cover I got whipped with a rod by a girl!)*

It wasn't in Jared's nature to sulk. But that was
exactly what he'd been doing since that little revealing chat with Kristi two days ago.

She'd loved him.

And he'd broken her heart.

He'd seen it in her wounded expression, the vulnerable glimmer in her eyes, and the more she'd pushed him for answers he couldn't give, the more he'd rebelled, desperate to push her away.

Hell, if he'd known how cut up she was about their break-up he never would've agreed to have her here on the island. He would've made Elliott choose an unknown, someone he had no hope of sharing a spark with.

And that was what annoyed him the most; the fact that all the denials in the world didn't change the fact that he was still attracted to her.

Just attracted?

Therein lay the kicker.

As long as he convinced himself it was a purely physical thing, an attraction for a beautiful woman, he could handle this, though deep down he knew better.

He might have grown up avoiding reality, doing his best to lose himself in tennis, but the longer he spent with Kristi, the longer he got to hear her sweet laugh and spar with her and try to elicit those amazing, uplifting smiles she did so well, the harder it was to deny the truth.

That she was right.

He was invested.

And not just in the rec centre.

'You ready to go down in another challenge?'

He stopped, wiggled his backpack higher, hands on hips. 'You just got lucky.'

She held up her hand, counted off her triumphs. 'In the water. While fishing. About to add reaching the top of this mountain first.'

'You think?'

'I know.'

Her self-righteous smirk had him wanting to cross the short distance between them and kiss that smug smile right off her gorgeous face.

'Pride before a fall and all that.'

She waved away his corny cliché. 'Let's just get this show on the road so I can cement my place as the virtual winner.'

He laughed at her audacity, a small part of him hoping she'd win. If he won he'd planned on donating the money to the centre anyway and in the grand scheme of things it wouldn't make much difference considering how much he'd already invested.

But for her to be here, putting up with everything he threw at her, she must really want the money, bad.

He shifted, winced at a slight stab in his reconstructed knee, unprepared for her quick shift from cocky to concerned, the flare of pity in her eyes obvious as her gaze zeroed in on his leg.

'You sure your knee can hold up to this?'

'I'm fine.'

His annoyed grunt could've been misconstrued for pain, but the only ache giving him any grief was the one in the vicinity of his heart.

He'd tried to stay away from her the last few days, tried to ease back into polite small talk and away from anything too personal, but, damn, he missed their closeness, missed seeing her tentative smiles as she slowly opened up to him again.

She narrowed her eyes, dropped her gaze to his knee before pinning him with an accusatory glare.

'Make sure you tell me if you need to rest.'

Hitching his backpack higher on his shoulders, he said, 'You'll be the one begging for a rest.'

Her mouth twitched at his quip as he silently pleaded for one of her brilliant smiles.

'You sportsmen are all the same.'

She fell into step beside him, trudging up the gentle incline, the twang in his chest having little to do with the increasing gradient and more to do with her being involved with other sportsmen.

'Speaking from personal experience?'

'Uh-huh.'

She didn't elaborate, tugging her ghastly floppy flamingo-pink hat lower so he couldn't see her face bar a few shadows.

'Pros?'

His fingers dug into the straps anchoring his

backpack, the thought of Kristi anywhere near some of the sleazebags he'd toured with making him want to punch the nearest tree.

He only just caught her mumbled, 'More like amateurs.'

He should leave well enough alone, had no right to delve into her past. But some curious demon egged him on, demanding answers he knew he wouldn't like.

'Old boyfriends?'

'Old fiancés.'

Her feet picked up speed while he stood rooted to the spot, shock ricocheting through him.

'Whoa!'

She stopped, turned, her face in shadow. 'What? You need a rest already?'

Broaching the short distance between them, he whipped off her hat.

'What I need is to hear more about these fiancés, *plural*?'

She shrugged, her expression carefully blank. 'I was engaged. Twice.'

She said it as if she'd been to the grocery store, twice, as if it was of little importance, a mundane occurrence, as boring as picking up a loaf of bread.

While he still reeled from the shock she snatched her hat out of his hand, rammed it back on her head.

'Any other questions?'

'Why didn't you go through with it, both times?'

He held his breath. What was wrong with him? Did he expect her to say because of him? Did he want her to?

That would be a bloody nightmare, something he couldn't bear to have on his conscience: that she'd once cared so much for him she couldn't go through with a marriage to another guy.

'You really want to know why?'

She flipped the brim back on her hat, raised an eyebrow in challenge, as if taunting him to admit the truth.

That while he wanted to hear her answer, it also terrified him.

Squaring his shoulders, he nodded. 'Wouldn't have asked if I didn't.'

Staring directly into his eyes, she said, 'With Avery and Barton, I mistook caring for love. And I'd never settle for anything but love. An all-consuming, blinding, passionate, no-holds-barred love.'

The scoffing sound he made had her smiling, a smug, patronising smile, as if she pitied him.

'Let me guess. You don't believe in it.'

'Damn straight. No such thing.'

Shaking her head, she said, 'I've seen it first-hand. Believe me, it exists.'

And he'd seen the exact opposite firsthand: a

bitter, twisted version of the embroidered emotion love, the likes of which still left him reeling and avoiding it at all costs.

He waved away her explanation. 'Where? With your friends? People think they're in love, go all soft and soppy, spouting it to anyone who'll listen, but behind closed doors they probably hate each other's guts and take it out on those around them.'

Something in his voice must've alerted her he spoke from experience as he silently cursed his wayward tongue.

This was about her, damn it, not him.

'You never talk about your past.'

Yep, she'd honed in on the one area that was off limits, to everyone.

'There's a reason why it's called the past. It needs to stay there.'

This time he kept walking, leaving her standing in the dust, but not for long. He should've known she wouldn't give up so easily.

'My parents had the perfect marriage.'

'No such thing as perfect.'

He didn't break stride, ignoring the twinge of guilt as she all but ran to keep up with him.

'Their love was amazing. Eyes only for each other. Totally besotted. It's the type of love I want.'

'Good luck with that,' he said, all this talk of

love and marriage almost as unpalatable as the thought of her loving two jerks called Avery and Barton enough to want to marry them.

'What about you?'

'What about me?'

'Any special someones over the last eight years?'

'Nope.'

'Too bad.'

He heard the underlying hint of glee in her tone, stopped and faced her.

'You sound happy about that.'

'None of my business.'

She waved a hand in front of her face, as if shooing a fly.

'Bet you would've been jealous if I had been.'

The amusement in her eyes faded, her mouth drooped. 'We've already established I cared back then. What do you want to do, ram the point home?'

'Hey, I was joking.'

He laid a hand on her arm and she shrugged it off, stepped away.

'Yeah, that's you, a regular joker.'

She stormed ahead, leaving him more bewildered than ever.

Women.

If they didn't have to reach the top of this hill to complete the hiking challenge and do a bit of preening in front of the cameras, he would've headed back to camp.

As he contemplated doing just that a scream pierced the air and his heart stopped as he saw the most infuriating woman on the planet go down in a heap ten metres ahead.

'Krissie!'

His knee gave a protesting twinge as he dumped his backpack and sprinted to where she'd gone down in an ungracious crumple. 'You okay?'

Sending him a withering glare, she winced as she moved her leg.

'Do I look okay?'

'Here, let me help.'

'Don't touch it!' She screamed as he reached out to assist her up.

'Your knee?'

'Ankle,' she snapped through gritted teeth, pain twisting her mouth, her face pale.

'I need to check it out.'

'Let me guess. You can add medico to your many talents.'

'That's Dr Malone to you,' he said, relieved when his lame humour elicited a wan smile. 'Where does it hurt?'

'Here.'

She pointed to the outside of her ankle, sporting a sizeable swelling already.

'Can you point your foot?'

She managed some degree of movement, cringing. 'Hurts like the devil.'

'Side to side?'

She cried out as she inverted her foot, made a grab for it and he stilled her arm with a touch.

'You've strained your lateral ligaments.'

His fingertips traced the swelling, gently probing, as he watched her face for reaction. 'Not broken, thank goodness.'

'Bet that would've sent Elliott's ratings sky-rocketing.'

'Stuff the ratings. I'm more concerned about you.'

'Careful. Concern could be confused with caring. And we both know you don't do that.'

'You'll live.'

He released her ankle, ready to spring up and flee as he usually did when emotions entered the conversation.

But something in her expression, an underlying vulnerability, a valiant bravado as she struggled to hide her pain, had him sinking back down to sit beside her, his heart sinking along with his body.

He'd known it would come to this.

All his denials, to her and himself, stood for jack in the face of this woman and what she brought to his life and what she made him feel.

'What do you want me to say? That you're right?'

He threw his hands up in the air in surrender. 'Fine. I care, damn it, I care. Happy now?'

'Getting there.'

Her radiant smile reached out to him, touched him in a way he'd never thought possible.

'Admitting that doesn't mean—'

'Shut up, Malone.'

She placed a hand over his mouth, her palm begging to be kissed. 'Quit while you're ahead.'

What was it about this woman that made him forget everything, made him forget why he couldn't feel, made him forget the pledge he'd made all those years ago?

As her hand slid from his mouth, along his jaw, and came to rest on the back of his neck before she tugged him forward and placed a soft, tender kiss on his lips, he knew.

She made him feel like a better man.

When he was with her, everything seemed brighter and shinier and lighter. It had been like that between them eight years ago and not much had changed.

The connection they shared was way beyond physical attraction; exactly why he'd done his best to deny it.

What if he didn't fight so hard?

Would that be so terrible?

'Stop thinking so much.'

He smiled against her mouth, eased away to stare into her sparkling blue eyes. 'Shouldn't that be my line?'

'No, your line is "where do we go from here?"'

'Right.'

Despite the banter between them, she'd honed in on what he was thinking.

Where *did* they go from here?

They had one night and one day to survive on the island, before back to reality. Was he prepared to start a relationship when he knew it couldn't go any further than casual dating? Would Kristi be up for that?

Her admittance of feelings for him first time around and her recent revelation of waiting for the perfect love should be enough to make him swim back to the mainland.

It didn't need to be so complicated. He'd be upfront from the start so she'd be under no false illusions. They'd date, have fun, nothing too heavy.

But what if she didn't go for it?

'First up, we go straight back down this mountain so I can tend to that ankle.'

Her eyes narrowed, not buying his brush-off for a second. 'How exactly do you propose to get me down there? Piggyback?'

'One better.'

Before she could argue he swept her into his arms, hoisting her in the air as he stood.

'Put me down, you great macho idiot. You'll ruin your knee!'

'I've been lifting weights ten times heavier than you,' he said, tightening his grip behind her knees as she started wriggling. 'And quit that, otherwise I'll drop you, you'll bruise your butt, and I'll have to tend to that too.'

Her mouth opened, closed, her lips compressed while her eyes sparked rebellious fire.

'You're enjoying this.'

'Damn straight.'

He couldn't look her in the eye, what with her face—and lips—within kissing distance, so he tightened his grip under her knees and concentrated on making it down the hill with his precious cargo.

To give her credit, she stopped wriggling and tightened her hold around his neck and for a crazy second he wanted to hold her like this, protect her, cherish her, for ever.

See, he knew admitting he cared was a dumb idea. Now he'd acknowledged the chink in his emotional armour, who knew what else he'd be forced to admit?

Such as how dating would be fun but being truly involved, emotionally invested, could change his life.

'You can put me down now.'

Distracted by his worrying thoughts, he'd made it down the last of the incline and reached their huts.

'Not 'til I get you in bed.'

Her choked sound had him chuckling. 'So I can tend to that ankle properly.'

'No need to clarify. I knew what you meant.'

Bumping the door to her hut open with his butt, he backed into the one-room abode, careful not to hit her head on the way through.

He paused on the threshold, his chest giving a painful twinge at the irony of holding this woman in his arms as he crossed into a room with the intention of getting her to bed.

'Don't worry, there were no vows involved.'

Another thing that scared him. She could read his mind, always could, seemed to know him better than he knew himself.

'And there never will be, not in this lifetime,' he said, crossing the sparse room to gently deposit her on the bed. 'Now sit tight while I grab some ice.'

'Yes, sir.'

She saluted, her eyes twinkling, her mouth curved into a tempting smile and, suddenly, that ice wasn't a bad idea. Not for her ankle though. There were parts of him in desperate need of cooling.

'Lucky there are no cameras in here,' he said,

rummaging through the mini freezer for ice, wrapping cubes in a tea towel and heading back to the bed.

'Nothing to do with luck.'

She winced as he elevated her foot with a rolled towel and settled the ice pack over the swelling. 'Having cameras out there for a few hours a day is bad enough. No way would I have done this if they were in my face twenty-four-seven.'

She shuffled forwards, rearranged the pillows behind her back, before sagging against the headboard. 'I'm not some media hound who loves the attention.'

'And I am?'

Shrugging, she plucked at the horrible brown chenille bedspread. 'There must be other ways to get publicity for the centre. Maybe you miss being in the spotlight?'

Silently cursing, he stood, started pacing the room, belatedly realising she was studying his every move.

Dropping into a chair nearby, he crossed his ankles, leaned back, hands clasped behind his head, his posture deliberately relaxed when nothing about this situation was remotely relaxing.

He didn't want to discuss how much he missed the spotlight or why. Kristi was too perceptive, too good at seeing right through him, and if he gave her a glimpse into his insight who knew what she'd uncover?

'You're in PR, you know what grabs kids' attention these days. Media. Social networking.'

'Hence our blogs and Twitter. Yeah, I get that. But why this? Why you? There must be directors and counsellors and any number of staff who could raise the profile. What do you get out of it? And don't tell me it's the prize money, because a hundred grand would be pocket change to you.'

The truth hovered on the tip of his tongue before he swallowed it, the lingering urge to unburden a sign of how close he'd come to blowing it.

She couldn't learn the truth, not all of it.

'Nothing too complicated. I just wanted to squeeze as much free publicity for the centre as possible. You know how much prime-time TV ads cost. Worth every second I'm here.'

'Very noble of you.'

Her eyes narrowed, assessing, and, while she didn't probe further, he knew by the astute gleam she hadn't entirely bought his story.

'Speaking of the cameras, we need to do a Twitter update. I'll grab my phone.'

Eager to escape, he strode to the door.

'Jared?'

'Yeah?'

With his hand on the doorknob, he paused, glanced over his shoulder, surprised by the vulnerable edge to her voice.

'Thanks for taking care of me.'

Thanks for caring about me, was what she really meant and, with a terse nod, he bolted.

Twitter.com/Stranded_Jared
Admitting the truth can't be good.

Twitter.com/Stranded_Kristi
Sprained ankle bearable, tension not. Last night on island. Escape can't come quick enough.

CHAPTER TEN

Stranded *Survival Tip #10*
Don't hang a 'Sex instructor: First lesson free'
sign on your hut.

KRISTI'S BLOG, DAY 6
Hiking challenge didn't happen. Made it a
quarter of the way up a very slight slope be-
fore my klutz gene kicked in and I fell. Didn't
help my pride it happened while storming
away from Jared in a huff. Though wasn't all
bad. Got him to admit he cared. Shock, horror!
  On the downside, that's another challenge
I've fluffed so I'm two from four. For my new-
found fans reading this, please don't bail now.
I need your continued hits! Keep the faith. I'm
going to win this comp if I have to swim back
to the mainland to do it. Maybe could feed my
opponent to the sharks while I'm at it?

JARED'S BLOG, DAY 6
So much for plan to keep distance from Kristi.

While her sprain better, she's still hobbling around and I can't abandon her. Cooking her dinner at her 'place'. Will make sure she's comfortable then leave.

Must repeat that last word several times for good measure, for I'm having decidedly 'un-leave-worthy' thoughts...

'YOU make a mean grilled cheese sandwich.'

Kristi patted her stomach and Jared's gaze followed the movement, lingered, before he leapt from the table on the pretext of clearing dishes.

'I'm a man of many talents. Didn't you know?'

She grunted a response and he wondered what it would take to get her to lighten up.

He'd been cheerful over dinner, flippant, had aimed for casual, fun, wanting to give her a glimpse of how good they'd once been together without all the heavy stuff they'd discussed the last few days.

For he'd come to a decision while he'd carried her down that mountain.

He'd already admitted he cared.

He enjoyed being with her.

He wanted to get to know her again, to date when they got back to Sydney.

But how to convince her when he'd done everything in his power while on the island to hide the real him, to evade her questions, to keep up the pretence that he hadn't changed from that young, fun-loving guy?

He had one night left. He'd make it count if it killed him.

While he rinsed the dishes, she wriggled around on the hard wooden dining chair, tentatively moving her ankle propped on another. Thanks to regularly changing ice packs and elevating it, the swelling had decreased significantly.

She could probably hobble on it, but with him attending to her every whim, where was the fun in that?

Sneaky? Too right. He liked having her dependent on him, having her ask him for help. It soothed his macho soul and went a small way to making up for the last few days.

Another reason he wanted tonight to be special. He had no idea where things stood between them once they returned to Sydney and if the next twenty-four hours were all he had with her, if she didn't go for his dating plan, he'd make every second count.

Stacking the dishes on the side sink, he dried his hands, bending over to grab a tea towel to do so, and heard a muffled groan.

Maybe she was in more pain than she'd let on. Yet when he straightened, turned, her gaze hastily shifting from his butt, he knew her sound had more to do with the tension buzzing between them than any sprain.

Good, time to liven things up a little. Grinning, he thrust his hands into his pockets and leaned against the sink.

'Fancy dessert?'

'What's on offer?'

He watched her eyes widen as she focused on his naughty smile as he pushed off the sink, crossed the small room to squat beside her chair.

'What do you want?'

Her fingers clung to the edge of her chair as he willed her to release them and reach out to his forearm resting near her bare thigh.

Static electricity crackled between them as he shifted a fraction, brushed her thigh, her slight jump nothing on the kick-start to his libido.

He held his breath, wishing she'd take a chance, wanting her to make the first move. After all he'd done in the past, all they'd been through, he couldn't push her; it wouldn't be fair.

'Got any more of that Swiss chocolate?'

'Sure.'

He stood and turned away, disappointed. Then again, what did he expect? For her to forget how he'd treated her and come back for seconds?

'Back in a sec.'

'Okay.'

There was something in her voice…a hint of mischief…and as he paused at the door, shot a quick glance over his shoulder and caught her perving on his butt again, he knew it was time to re-evaluate the situation.

Maybe Kristi wasn't so indifferent to the idea of making this night special?

If that was the case, he had high plans for Miss Wilde and the fine chocolate when he returned. High plans indeed.

Jared thumped around his hut, grabbed his backpack and dumped the contents on the table. He'd clean up the mess later. Something he'd have to do with his life if he continued down this suicidal path.

Spying the chocolate, he left it sitting amidst the mess, jammed his hand through his hair and started pacing.

What the hell was he doing?

He'd played this game with Kristi before, pretending their relationship was oh-so-casual, deliberately ignoring the signs she cared too much.

That twinkle in her eye as he'd left her cabin proved how much she cared, for he knew she'd never consider getting physical unless she was emotionally invested.

She'd told him that first time around and he'd gone ahead and taken advantage of the situation, a young guy crazy for a beautiful woman. He'd kidded himself back then, ignored the signs she cared more than he did, content to coast along, have fun.

But he wasn't that young guy any more. He was wiser, more mature, knew how much it must've cost her to finally let down her guard and give him that monkey-business look.

So where did that leave his plan to make their last night together on the island special?

Basically, he couldn't keep his hands off her.

She was injured, for goodness' sake! Yet he'd taken every opportunity to touch her, on the pretext of helping her.

Probing her ankle? Yep.

Scooping her into his arms to move her from the bed to the chair? Yep.

Skimming her shapely calf while settling her ankle on a cushion? Done that too.

Sick.

Now he had to march back over there and do it all again, helping her from the chair to the bed, tucking her in, making sure she was comfortable…

Two words stuck in his head, on repeat.

The bed…the bed…the bed…

He wanted to be in that bed with her so badly he ached.

But they hadn't talked yet, hadn't established

boundaries about their new relationship and maybe now wasn't the time despite the urge to march back there and lay everything out. He wanted her fighting fit, in full possession of her faculties, painkiller free, so that she couldn't blame any misconceptions on a fogged head.

Listen to yourself. Making excuses for the relationship before it's even begun.

'It's what I do.'

Admit it. Kristi's different. You care. And that scares the hell out of you.

'Damn straight. I don't want to hurt her.'

Is she the only one you're scared of hurting? You're really screwed up since the injury and the fiasco with your parents.

'Shut up.'

Tired of arguing with himself, he snatched several Swiss chocolate bars and headed back to Kristi's hut.

He had no idea what to do about their situation but he'd been under pressure before, had always come out on top.

He'd figure it out. If not, he'd fall back on the old fail-safe that had got him through every convoluted part of his life.

Wing it.

'What do you think you're doing?'

Kristi, propped on her good leg, sent Jared a

sheepish smile as he burst through the door. 'Testing out my ankle.'

'Testing my patience, more like it.'

He dumped the chocolate on the table and scooped her into his arms before she could utter a word of protest.

Not that she would have. She was enjoying this whole invalid thing far too much for comfort.

'You really don't have to carry me.'

As he smiled down at her, his face mere inches from hers, she tried to think of every sane reason why he shouldn't, for right this very moment she could think of nowhere else she'd rather be than in his arms.

'Would you rather I slung you over my shoulder like a sack of spuds?'

'Brute.'

'Hey, would a brute do this?'

He lowered her gently to the bed, placed a cushion under her ankle, arranged the pillows behind her, her heart careening out of control and slamming against her chest wall with him in such close proximity.

She knew what he'd do next.

Hand her the chocolate. Pass her the latest romantic suspense novel she'd brought. And leave.

Not while she still had a breath in her body.

Staying aloof, maintaining a cool front, keeping her distance, had slowly but surely driven her insane.

She'd wanted closure when she first arrived here? She'd partially got her wish, with him apologising and acknowledging he cared. But as long as her body craved him, confusing her mind with mixed messages, she'd never have full closure, not the way she wanted.

So while he'd gone in search of chocolate, she'd searched her heart, her mind, and come to a decision. Only one way to get the closure she needed to move on with her life since he'd re-entered it.

Get him out of her system once and for all.

As he straightened she captured his hand. 'You're not a brute, far from it.'

His gaze clashed with hers, searching, wary, and she tugged so hard he had no option but to sit on the bed beside her.

'Krissie, don't go building me up into some-one I'm not.'

'I'm not a naïve young woman any more. I know what I'm doing.'

His reserved expression softened. 'Do you? Really?'

This was it.

The point of no return.

Every tension-filled minute over the last week,

every loaded smile, every flirtatious quip, had been leading to this and her body tingled in anticipation.

Releasing his hand, her fingertips trailed up his arm, across his shoulder, dipping between his collarbones, before resting on his lips, tracing the contours while she moistened her own with her tongue.

Sliding her hand around the back of his neck, she pulled him slowly towards her.

'I know exactly what I'm doing,' she murmured, a second before she kissed him.

His resistance was fleeting, the merest rigidity in his shoulders before his arms wrapped around her and he kissed her with as much passion, as much desperation as she reciprocated, a frantic, explosive kiss filled with hunger and longing and soul-deep need.

His lips left hers all too soon, trailing across to her ear, where he whispered, 'What about your ankle?'

'I won't need my ankle, unless you've turned kinky over the last eight years.'

His joyous laughter burst over her like a warm spring shower and she laughed along with him, their intimacy having more to do with the past they'd shared than shedding their clothes, a long, leisurely, exploratory process that left her trembling by the time they were naked.

'You're so beautiful.'

His hand hovered over her hip as he stared at her, his eyes gleaming with desire before he splayed his hand flat against her belly and she gasped at the heat from his palm branding her his.

'And you still have the power to drive me wild.'

As his hand skated across her skin, exploring, teasing, tantalising, she lost herself in the exquisite rapture, in the pleasure, in the absolute certainty that despite wanting closure, she'd just opened her heart to Jared Malone again.

Twitter.com/Stranded_Jared
What have I done?

Twitter.com/Stranded_Kristi
So much for closure. Start of a beautiful new…day.

CHAPTER ELEVEN

Stranded *Survival Tip #11*
Sharing the last piece of beef jerky is only polite.

KRISTI'S BLOG, DAY 7
The last day on the island passed in a blur of interviews, cameras and fake smiles, when all I wanted to do was smile for real. In fact, from the moment I woke to find Jared's note, I couldn't keep the grin off my face. Then Elliott and the media descended and I didn't have a minute to myself. Worse, I didn't have a chance to talk to Jared in private. That's where the fake smiles came in. We acted very chummy, sparring with each other on camera, smiles firmly fixed in place. But what was he thinking? Really thinking behind that smile? I intend to find out. Today.

Oh, and hoping my soldiering-on-under-duress routine was enough to win the hundred grand!

JARED'S BLOG, DAY 7
Up and at 'em early this morning, in time for
the media circus. Did the usual meet-and-
greet stuff. Great publicity for 'Activate'.
Looking forward to seeing what's been hap-
pening at the centre in my absence.

'Your blog entries were short and sweet.'

Jared drummed his fingers against the table,
reached for his latte, pushed it away again, his
eyes firmly fixed on the door.

'I'm a bloke. What did you expect?'

Elliott's sly grin alerted him to a veer in topic
he wouldn't like.

'Kristi's were interesting.'

'Yeah?'

He grabbed at the latte this time, gulped the lot,
scorching his tongue in the process. Good, as he
had no intention of discussing Kristi or what
happened on Lorikeet Island with his mate.

'Now that you're back, maybe you should
read them.'

'Too busy.'

He slammed the glass on the table, glanced at
his watch, wishing he could beg off this post-
island-wrap-up. He didn't want the first time he
saw Kristi to be here, like this.

She deserved more. She deserved an explanation.

Or maybe that should be a clarification. For while they'd done the deed last night they hadn't had a chance to talk, really talk, about where things stood.

And that worried him. He didn't want her getting any crazy ideas.

He wasn't a complete fool. He'd seen the starry-eyed look in her eyes when they'd faced the media, had felt her subtle adoration like a hit over the back of the head with a tennis racket.

While his pulse pounded at the memory of their hot encounter, and the driving need to do it all again, he needed to set boundaries.

'Relax, she'll be here.'

His gaze snapped from the door to Elliot as he deliberately sat back.

'Of course she will. She's a professional.'

'Is that all she is?'

Sending Elliott a glare he'd used to intimidate opponents—considering his record it had worked most of the time—he folded his arms.

'Kristi's a trouper. She handled all those bogus challenges you set up for us, she acted accordingly in front of the cameras to boost *your* ratings—'

'What about when the cameras were off?'

Off camera had been the time he'd enjoyed the most, when she'd slipped off her bubbly PR face and relaxed into the lively, carefree girl he'd known.

He'd dated extensively over the years, had

squired movie stars and supermodels and sporting legends to glittering affairs from Monte Carlo to New York, but none of those women could capture his imagination as much as Kristi Wilde in all her natural, vivacious glory.

Elliott held up his hand. 'On second thoughts, don't answer that. I can see your response written all over your face.'

Hoping like crazy his mate couldn't see half of what he was thinking, he deliberately relaxed his shoulders, uncrossed his arms.

'And what's that?'

'Tennis's notorious bachelor boy has fallen.'

'Bull.'

Shoving his glasses up his nose, Elliott leaned across the table, peered into Jared's face as if scrutinising a particularly challenging Sudoku puzzle.

'Nope. No bull. You get this funny look in your eyes whenever I mention her, then there's that goofy grin you had on the island this morning, and you're never tight-lipped about any of your other conquests—'

'She's not a conquest!'

He slammed his palms on the table, rattling the cutlery, sloshing water from glasses, annoyed as hell at Elliott's knowing smirk.

'Well, well, well, I think your reaction settles that particular question.'

'Smart ass.'

Chuckling, Elliott flipped open his laptop. 'Smart? Yeah. An ass? Not so much.'

Elliott was right. He was the ass. And far from smart if he overreacted at the mere thought of Kristi being anything more to him than a casual girlfriend.

It had all sounded so simple when he'd mentally rehearsed how to handle this relationship. So why was he getting so hot and bothered now?

He'd survived being raised by two narcissists who made boxing championships look like toddlers sparring.

He'd survived being dumped at the tennis club from an early age.

He'd survived his career falling apart when he'd gone down in that twisted, tangled heap on Centre Court at Flushing Meadow.

Surely he could handle one fiery, opinionated woman, no matter how tempting?

'Don't look now but your *friend* has arrived.'

Elliott's not so subtle emphasis on friend earned him another death glare as Jared snuck a quick peek at the door.

So much for quick. The instant Kristi strutted into Icebergs, all legs in a tight black mini dress and killer shoes, a coy smile playing about the mouth he remembered in minute, erotic detail, he couldn't tear his gaze away.

She zeroed in on him, her smile widening as she raised a hand in greeting and something deep down, in a place he didn't acknowledge these days let alone indulge, twanged. Hard.

'She's great.'

'Yeah.'

He couldn't look away, mesmerised by the sway of her hips as she wound her way between the tables, hypnotised by the mischievous shimmer in her blue eyes, as if she had a secret and he was in on it.

Clenching his hands under the table, he inhaled, trying to stay cool when all he wanted to do was leap from his chair, vault the tables and sweep her into his arms.

'You should see the footage. Priceless.'

'Yeah?'

Jared couldn't care less about the documentary footage. All he cared about this very minute was having Kristi sit next to him, her seductive spicy scent enveloping him, reminding him of how close they'd got last night, how her scent had clung to him all morning despite an early shower to clear his head.

'Hey, boys. Haven't we done this before?'

She slid into a chair, dumped her monstrous handbag and signalled a waiter, ordering a soy chai latte while beaming at them.

He loved that about her. Her energy, her pizzazz, her zest for life.

His use of the L word pinged in his brain a second too late and before he could process it she clapped her hands together.

'So, Mr Producer, how did we do? And more importantly, who won?'

Elliott tapped his laptop screen. 'Pure gold. I'm almost done editing and splicing the footage, should have it ready for you to view tomorrow.'

She batted her eyelashes and something twisted inside as he registered Elliott's goofy expression. Not that he could blame the guy. He was only human and what red-blooded male wouldn't be affected by Kristi Wilde at her flirtatious best?

'As for the winner, I've tallied your individual site hits.'

Elliott paused for drama and Jared rolled his eyes.

Taking hold of Kristi's hand, Elliott bowed over it while Jared clubbed the green-eyed monster making him want to box his friend's ears.

'I'm pleased to announce that you, my dear, are the winner.'

Kristi's loud whoop had several nearby patrons craning their heads, frowns easing into patient smiles as they registered her infectious excitement.

'Bloody brilliant!' She pumped her fist in the air, the action drawing his attention to the black dress pulling deliciously across her breasts. 'Thanks so much.'

Elliott grinned like a proud benefactor. 'My pleasure.'

'Congratulations.'

She turned her triumphant smile on him and the impact slugged him all the way to his toes.

With a toss of her hair, she licked the tip of her finger and chalked one up in the air. 'Never in doubt.'

He chuckled, leaned towards her and whispered loudly behind his hand, 'I could've whipped your butt if I'd wanted.'

Holding her hand in his face, she said, 'Talk to this.'

Elliott joined in their laughter at the antics while Jared desperately tried to subdue the wave of longing swamping him.

Last night had achieved what he'd feared most. Opened his heart to Kristi all over again. Left him wanting more. Much more than what they'd shared last time.

'So where to from here? Are you doing a special preview screening just for us?'

Elliott blushed as she added a beguiling smile to the mix.

'And any family and close friends you'd like to bring along.'

Her smile slipped a fraction, but enough for him to recognise the loss of her parents must've hit her hard. Divulging their idyllic marriage to him on the island explained a lot. Her quest for love, for the perfect man, for marriage, all centred on what she'd grown up with.

Which went a long way to explaining his own aversion to the institution.

The marriage he'd been privy to was filled with screaming matches and vitriol and abuse; emotional, psychological, worse than physical.

His parents had been ratbags, certainly not cut out for parenthood and, while he acknowledged not every marriage was a trial, he'd seen enough to know the whole ''til death us do part' thing was not for him.

'I'll bring my sister, Meg, and my boss, Ros. They'll get a laugh out of it.'

Pathetically eager to bustle in on the conversation between the two, Jared leaned his forearms on the table. 'Surely my acting wasn't that bad?'

Her eyes twinkled as she turned towards him, the impact of her dazzling smile hitting him in the chest as only a smile from her could.

'Acting? You mean you were acting all those times you preened and ponced around in front of the cameras?'

She crooked her finger at Elliott, who practically fell over himself trying to lean across the table.

'Have you seen the part where he erected the tents? And gathered wood? And built a bonfire? True he-man stuff. All that posing and muscle flexing had to be staged.'

Elliott grinned, rubbed his hands together. 'You should see the footage now. I've added sound effects and music and—'

'Can you two quit it? You're giving me a complex.'

'That'll be the day.'

Her cute scoff formed her lips into a delicious pout, instantly transporting him back to last night and exactly what she'd done with those talented lips.

The thought had him reaching for his water and draining the entire glass in four gulps.

Elliott closed his laptop. 'Seriously, you two did a great job. Your blogs and Twitter updates have generated loads of talk and interest, so the public are hankering for our official screening next week.'

Elliott reached into his top pocket, pulled out an envelope, handed it to Kristi.

'Here's your cheque. Money well spent if I get

another gong for the documentary and guaranteed funding for my next project.'

'Thanks.'

Kristi quickly slipped her cheque into the bag at her feet, but not before Jared had seen the sheen of tears.

Though she hadn't told him what she'd do with the money if she won, he'd bet she'd share some of it. She was that type of person, had a generous heart, a heart he had no intention of breaking this time around, clear warning they had to have a 'talk' before this thing between them went any further.

Sculling the soy chai latte that had been placed in front of her while they'd been chatting, Kristi leaped from her chair, hooked her bag over her shoulder and darted a quick glance at the door.

'It's been a blast, guys, but I have to get back to work.'

Not wanting to let her go so soon, not before they'd had a chance to talk privately, Jared stood.

'It's your first day back and almost four. Surely you can skive off the rest of the day?'

Annoyance contorted her mouth before she slipped a smile back in place. 'No, sorry, gotta go.'

Grabbing her arm before she bolted, he leaned down to murmur in her ear.

'We haven't had a chance to talk after last night.'

'Call me later.'

She tried to twist out of his grasp but he held firm. 'Are you okay? You seemed fine with Elliott but now—'

'I have to get back to work.'

He couldn't hang onto her without causing a scene and he reluctantly released her. Before she could take a step he swooped down for a snatched kiss, his lips meeting hers all too briefly before she stepped away, staring at him with bemusement, shock and just a little fear.

'I'll call you,' he said, holding her answering tremulous smile close to his heart.

When she'd gone, he finally registered he was still standing, while Elliot lounged back in his chair with an aggravatingly patronising smile on his smug face.

'Well, I guess that answers my question.'

Reluctantly taking a seat, he said, 'What question's that?'

Elliott's grin broadened. 'The one about what happened off camera.' He snapped his fingers. 'And the one about bachelor boy falling.'

'Shut up.'

Elliott toasted him with water. 'I won't say another word. Besides, you'll see for yourself once you take a look at the footage.'

Ignoring the niggle of foreboding he'd let on

more than he'd wanted to on the island, Jared suddenly couldn't wait for the pre-screening of Elliott's masterpiece.

CHAPTER TWELVE

Stranded *Survival Tip #12*
The camera never lies.

> *Twitter.com/Stranded_Jared*
> *Good to be back to civilisation.*

> *Twitter.com/Stranded_Kristi*
> *Christian Louboutin, oh, how I love thee.*
> *Can you tell I missed my shoes?*

'SINCE when did you become addicted to Twitter?'

'Since the island.'

Kristi barely glanced at Meg as she slipped her mobile into her handbag, wishing Jared's last tweet had been more informative.

'So I have tennis boy to thank for moving you into the twenty-first century?'

'He may have had something to do with it.'

Along with fast-tracking her heart forward

eight years and landing her right back where she'd been when they'd first met.

Star-struck. Mooning. Just a tad in love.

She'd had it confirmed the second she'd entered Icebergs two hours ago, locked gazes with him and lost her breath. They'd only been apart a few hours and the heavy weight of missing him pressing on her chest had lifted the moment she'd seen him sitting oh-so-casually at the table.

It had little to do with a white polo shirt hugging a broad chest, muscular arm draped across the back of his chair or the model-handsome face that had broken hearts of sports fans across the globe, and everything to do with his sense of humour, his sense of honour, his sense of decency.

He made her laugh, he made her cry; with the yearning to get to really know him and, hope-fully, keep him in her life this time. For ever.

'Did you two get it on?'

Used to Meg's bluntness, she picked up her sangria, raised the glass in her sister's direction. 'Oops. Did I fail to mention private details of my sex life on Twitter? Silly me.'

Meg chuckled, clinked glasses. 'Ah-ha! So there was sex involved?'

Kristi made a zipping motion across her lips.

Meg sculled half her glass, blinked her eyes at the sting of alcohol, before jabbing a finger at her.

'You better hope there weren't any hidden cameras in your room, that's all I can say.'

Dismissing her spurt of panic as irrational—Elliott would never do that to them—she sipped at her drink.

'Why not? After my documentary experience, I quite fancy a stint on YouTube.'

'You're insane.'

'Right back at you, sis.'

They grinned at each other, their closeness the one thing that had got her through their parents' death all those years ago.

The Bobbsey Twins, everyone had called them, and despite their age difference they'd been best friends and confidantes from a young age.

It irked what her sister went through every day, all because she'd been foolish enough to chase the same dream Kristi had: craving the perfect marriage, the perfect man, the perfect life. Sadly, in Meg's case, the dream became twisted, leaving her abandoned and pregnant without a wedding ring in sight.

While Jared had broken her heart eight years ago, at least she hadn't been left to raise a baby. Prue was adorable but raising a child didn't fit into her career plans right now.

Thanks to her stint on Lorikeet Island she could now give Meg and her adorable niece some much-needed help.

Reaching into her handbag, her fingers clasped the crisp envelope, pulled it out and handed it over.

'Here. This is for you.'

'What is it? A summons?'

'Better. Go on, open it.'

Meg ripped open the seal, withdrew the cheque, confusion creasing her brow as she scanned it, her eyes widening as she held it up to the light, reread it.

'It has my name on it.'

'That's because it's yours, silly.'

Meg's mouth opened and closed several times, before she dropped the cheque on the table as if burned.

'Don't be ridiculous.'

Picking up the cheque, she unfurled Meg's rigid fingers and pressed it back into her hand. 'It's yours. For you and Prue.'

Giving her sister a hug, and swallowing back tears, she said, 'Take it, Megs. Give that gorgeous girl everything her heart desires.'

'B-but it's a hundred grand!'

'I had to go without Christian Louboutin's latest black ostrich sandal and pitch a tent and suffer a sprained ankle for that money so you sure as hell better use it. I don't want my short-lived television debut to be in vain.'

Meg clutched at the cheque, stared at it for an

eternity, before flinging her arms around Kristi's neck.

'You're the best! How can I ever thank you?'

Squeezing Meg tight, she said, 'By being happy and continuing to do a fabulous job raising the cutest niece in the world.'

'I'll do my best.'

Meg hiccuped, sniffled, enough to set off her own crying jag.

'Hey, you're supposed to be doing cartwheels, not bawling.'

'Your fault.'

Meg pulled away, swiped at her nose, her eyes red and puffy. 'You sure about this? You can't use the money?'

'Apart from the promotion, the only reason I agreed to do *Stranded* was for a chance to win the money. I intended to give it to you all along.'

Kristi picked up their glasses, handed one to Meg. 'So drink up. And start planning. Maybe consider changing apartments? Invest some of it? An education fund? How about—?'

'Thanks, sis, I've got it covered.'

Kristi clamped her lips shut. 'I'll drink to that.'

As they sipped at their sangria and Meg's eyes took on a starry gleam, a tiny sliver of apprehension intruded on her magnanimous good feeling.

What if Meg chose to move interstate, where the

rentals were much cheaper? Rosanna was a good buddy but she was also her boss and Kristi had held back on loads of personal stuff in the past, not wanting to blur the lines and appear unprofessional.

She'd handled both break-ups with Avery and Barton in the same way: thrown herself into work, attended as many PR parties as humanly possible, filled her wardrobe with new shoes and hung out with Meg and Prue on the weekends.

What would she do this time?

That was her real worry, the expectation she'd break up with Jared and would have to deal with the devastation alone.

The thought had her sculling her drink, her hand shaky as she replaced the glass on the table.

'What's wrong?'

'Nothing,' she lied, not wanting anything to mar Meg's happiness.

'It's tennis boy, isn't it? You never did get around to telling me what happened on the island, what with waving six figures around and distracting me from the goss. How did the closure thing go?'

'Jury's still out on that.'

She could tell Meg nothing, or she could give her the abbreviated version. 'He hasn't changed a bit. Still charming. Still gorgeous.'

'Still has the power to reduce you to mush.'

Kristi nodded ruefully. 'That too.'

Peering over the rim of her glass, Meg mumbled, 'You know he's the love of your life, right? And the reason you didn't hook up with banker boy and number cruncher?'

Kristi laughed. 'Wish you'd called Avery and Barton those nicknames to their faces.'

'I did. Didn't help them get the message though.'

'What message?'

'The one where they didn't have a hope of getting you up the aisle because neither of them could hold a tennis racket.'

'You're harping.'

'I'm also dead right.'

That was the problem. Meg was one hundred per cent right and now she'd finally admitted—if only to herself—that she loved Jared, she could see it so clearly.

She'd given her all to both engagements, had been emotionally invested, had wanted to love Avery and Barton with all her heart. They'd been great guys, cute and reliable and steady.

And not a patch on a charming, confident playboy tennis pro with a hint of something dark and dangerous beneath his smooth veneer.

Had she tried hard enough with Avery and Barton? She'd thought so at the time but something they'd both said niggled... 'Can any guy live up to your expectations?'

Maybe they'd got it right? Maybe she'd been subconsciously comparing them to Jared? Then again, Jared hadn't lived up to expectations either, dumping her in favour of his career.

She'd worked through her guilt at ending both engagements, had analysed them to death. Maybe this time round with Jared, she could put some of what she'd learned to good use?

'You need to talk to him, sis. Make it clear what you want from the start.' Meg patted her cheek. 'You don't get many second chances in a lifetime. Better make the most of this one.'

Kristi had every intention to.

When she plucked up the courage to tell him she'd been foolish enough to fall for him, again.

'You've been avoiding me.'

Kristi jumped as Jared whispered in her ear, taking advantage of their proximity, inhaling her sweet, spicy scent that evoked so many visceral reactions his gut clenched.

'Shh. The documentary's about to start.'

'That's not an answer.'

He vaulted the sofa and plopped into the empty space beside her, desperate to talk after reading her blog and Twitter entries from Lorikeet Island.

They revealed so much and after what had

happened their last night on the island…yep, they definitely needed to talk.

'Should you be doing that with your knee?'

Flexing it to prove a point, he said, 'As I recall, my bung knee held up just fine on the island. It was your dodgy ankle that made you wimp out of the hiking challenge.'

'I didn't wimp out! I was injured, you unfeeling—'

He kissed her before she could say another word, a quick, brief kiss that barely lasted a second but enough contact to sizzle his synapses.

'That always was the best way to shut you up,' he murmured as Elliott strode into the room, closely followed by two women.

'You'll keep.'

She bumped him with her shoulder, shared an intimate smile that reminded him so much of the past his chest ached. They'd been in sync back then and he fervently wished they could slip back into an easy-going relationship.

After reading her blog entries, he didn't know what to think. One particular entry stuck in his head.

Problem is, have tried this before, eight years ago to be precise. Didn't work then, what makes me think it'll work now? He's closed up tight.

He cared about Kristi, wanted to give them a shot but if he didn't open up, tell her all of it, would she have a bar of him?

He'd spent a lifetime suppressing his childhood memories, channelling all his energy and frustrations into whacking a ball around a court.

He didn't know what he feared most. Feeling too much for her or opening up an old wound to find he hadn't healed at all. Or, worse, what she might think of him because of it.

They had to talk. When he'd called last night, she'd let it go through to her message bank, probably too physically and emotionally drained to face him yet. Not that he could blame her.

Spending the week with her had seriously disturbed his equilibrium and he'd needed space to think, time to figure out what he wanted to say before blurting the truth and ruining any chance they had before they really got started.

Nudging her right back, he jerked a thumb at the two women standing in front of them, knowing grins making them look like twin cats that'd swallowed an aviary of canaries.

'Introductions?'

'Jared. Meet Meg, my sister.'

'Nice to meet you.'

He stood, shook Meg's hand and bent to kiss

her on the cheek, a gesture that registered approval if Kristi's wide grin was any indication.

'Krissie's told me a lot about you.' Meg smirked, and Kristi shook her head in warning, only serving to stir Meg up. 'Your past together and—'

'And this is Ros, my boss.'

He laughed at her diversion, sending her a wink for good measure.

Pumping his hand, Rosanna pursed her Botoxed lips. 'If you're ever in need of a new PR firm, you know who to call.'

By the predatory sparkle in Rosanna's greedy gaze, PR wasn't the only reason she hoped he'd call. While he hated the term 'cougar' for older women dating younger men, there was something about Rosanna and the way she eyeballed him as prime devouring material that made the analogy apt.

'Thanks, I'll keep that in mind.'

He pulled out nearby chairs for Meg and Rosanna before resettling beside Kristi, his thigh brushing hers, the heat radiating from it sending an answering spark through his body.

Leaning across to whisper in her ear so the others couldn't hear, he said, 'What did you think of my blogs?'

'Typical.'

'Of what?'

She turned her head slightly, caution deepening

her eyes to sapphire. 'Of you bolting from anything resembling emotion.'

'Ouch.'

He clutched his heart, faked a smile when in fact her comment hit too close to home.

'But, hey, nothing I didn't know already, right?'

Her light tone hadn't changed but there was something in her eyes, a hint of vulnerability bordering on hurt that made him want to snatch her into his arms and never let go.

'Yours were rather revealing.'

She quickly averted her gaze as a blush stained her cheeks. 'Really? I didn't think they said much.'

'Oh, they said plenty.'

'Maybe you read too much into them?'

Unable to resist teasing her, he ran a fingertip across her collarbone, delighting in the instant pebbling of her skin beneath his touch.

'That's something I'd like to find out,' he murmured, brushing a soft kiss against her cheek.

'Ready?' Elliott rubbed his hands together, glanced at his captive audience, while Jared straightened, then sneaked a hand across and squeezed Kristi's knee in reassurance.

'Later,' he mouthed, relieved when she nodded and placed her hand on top of his.

Rosanna called out, 'Roll the tape, maestro,' as Jared slung an arm over the back of the sofa, his fingertips brushing Kristi's left shoulder, the soft smooth skin beckoning him to continue his exploration, sending blinding need pounding through him.

She leaned into him, snuggling, and as he tightened his grip he wondered what took him so long to figure out this felt right.

As their faces filled the projector screen Elliott had set up for the preview his contentment received a serious jolt.

There she was, on the first day, staring up at him as the boat pulled away, stranding them on Lorikeet Island.

And there he was, looking down on her, his adoring expression so open, so revealing, it snagged his breath in his lungs and held it there until he exhaled in a panicked whoosh.

Heck, if his feelings were that obvious—on the first day!—what would the rest of the documentary reveal?

Over the next hour he sat there, mortified with every passing minute, wondering if the public would see past her initial prickliness, her reticence, the arguments, his jokes, his deliberate flirting, and see what he saw.

A guy in love.

A guy so obviously in love he'd let the whole world know before telling the woman in question.

As the final credits rolled, and Meg and Rosanna hooted, whistled and broke into spontaneous applause, Jared removed his arm, sat up and stared straight ahead, his back ramrod straight, his face deliberately expressionless.

Hell.

Elliott switched on the lights, worry lines creasing his brow. 'Well, what do you think?'

'It's fantastic!'

Meg gave a thumbs-up of approval while Rosanna's eyes glittered with triumph.

'Pure gold,' Rosanna said, leaping up from her chair to grab Elliott's arm. 'Would you like me to put a PR package together for you? Because we're doing one for Channel Nine's new show shortly and…'

He tuned off, his senses on high alert, his attention focused on the woman beside him who hadn't said a word.

Picking up on the tension, Meg cast a worried glance their way before heading for the kitchen. 'I'll grab the pitcher of margaritas. Back in a minute.'

Jared didn't move, bracing his elbows on his knees, leaning forward, his gaze riveted to the screen, shell shocked.

After what seemed like an eternity, Kristi spoke. 'What did you think?'

He blew out a long, low breath, before finally turning to face her.

'I think we need to talk.'

'You're giving me the 'we need to talk' line?'

Her anger spiked in a second, her lips compressed, her eyes flashing fire, as he silently cursed his inability to comprehend what he was feeling let alone communicate it to the woman he loved.

The woman he loved.

Hell.

'I wanted to talk yesterday but you gave me the brush-off. Then last night you didn't answer your phone.'

Straightening as Meg re-entered the room and cast a curious glance their way, he lowered his tone. 'So, yeah, we need to talk. Whether you want to or not.'

Her shoulders slumped as she nodded. 'How soon can we beg off?'

Jerking his head towards Elliott, in his element surrounded by two beautiful women downing margaritas at a rate of knots, he said, 'Fifteen minutes should about do it for politeness. Then we're out of here.'

'You're on.'

Standing, Kristi headed towards the jolly three-some, while he sat there, stunned at what that tell-all documentary had revealed, trying to make sense of it all.

And wondering what the hell he was going to do about it.

CHAPTER THIRTEEN

Stranded *Survival Tip #13*
Falling coconuts not as dangerous as ones thrown at you in exasperation by fellow island inhabitants.

Twitter.com/Stranded_Jared
Been kidding myself. About everything.

Twitter.com/Stranded_Kristi
If the camera never lies, maybe it should tell a few fibs.

JARED knew this spot.

They used to come here all the time. Picnics by the harbour, wine at dusk, strolling along the water's edge hand in hand.

A good spot for what he had to say. If he could get the words straight in his head.

What he'd seen on that film hadn't just confused him; it had detonated every preconceived notion he'd ever had about love clear out of this world.

'I'm not interested in taking a stroll down memory lane.'

Jared stared out over Sydney Harbour, his gaze fixed on the lit bridge, his knee giving a twinge as he rocked on the balls of his feet.

'Neither am I.'

He turned to face her, hoping he didn't make a mess of this. 'I want to discuss our future.'

'Wow, that's a surprise.'

Kristi's voice held a dubious edge and he couldn't blame her. Last night, he'd been ready to lay it all out: them dating, having fun, nothing too heavy.

All that had changed since he'd seen Elliott's documentary. He could spout all he wanted about keeping their relationship casual, dating, hanging out, whatever he wanted to call it, but he knew without a doubt that however he dressed it up, Kristi would see right through him.

He loved her yet he didn't want to marry, ever.

Where did that leave him? Them?

What could he say without coming across as a selfish jerk who wanted her, just not enough?

If he hadn't seen the evidence with his own eyes, seen how much he loved her, sat through the excruciating hour of watching them interact on the island, his feelings etched on his face for the world to see, he wouldn't have believed it.

Though that was a crock and he knew it. There'd been signs on the island: the emotions she dredged up from deep within him, his admission he cared, the certainty that when she was with him, he was a better man.

All fine and good but if they reunited for real this time, she'd want more. She'd want it all, just as she'd hinted at when he'd walked in on her in that damn wedding dress.

He couldn't give her what she wanted and he shrivelled inside at the thought of breaking her heart all over again.

'Jared? About the documentary—'

'I know.'

A wary frown eased across her brow. 'You know what?'

'What it looked like.'

Even saying the words out loud squeezed his chest in a vice, tight, uncomfortable, strangling the very air from his lungs.

'Like…?'

'Don't.'

He held up a hand, jammed the other through his hair. 'We know each other too well to play these games.'

'I'm not—'

'I looked like an idiot.'

He pronounced it like a terminal condition. Exactly how he viewed the ludicrous emotion and all it stood for: control, competition, callousness.

He couldn't love.

It wasn't in his genetic make-up.

His father didn't have it: he'd spent his life at his precious men's club, only deeming to acknowledge his wife and child to hurl put-downs or abuse their way.

His mother didn't have it: she'd slept her way through the bridge club, the country club and the polo club before he'd won his first junior comp.

And neither of them had had the remotest love for him. Until he'd hit the big time, though their fawning couldn't be labelled as anything other than what it was: two people trying to cash in on his fame, playing the role of proud parents when in reality they didn't give a stuff.

The closest he'd come to feeling anything remotely resembling the ill-fated emotion was with Kristi eight years ago.

But even she'd disillusioned him at the end, putting her wishes ahead of his, placing him in that ludicrous position by making him choose between her or his career.

'I think you looked fine.'

She sat on the concrete wall edging the path

leading down to the harbour, her legs swinging, her face turned slightly to the right so he couldn't read her expression.

Reluctantly perching a foot away from her, he braced his hands on the wall.

'What do you want me to say?'

'Say what you think.'

He couldn't, not without telling her the truth about his past, not without revealing too much of himself and exposing a vulnerability he barely acknowledged existed.

'For goodness' sake, it shouldn't be this hard.'

She slid off the wall, dusted her butt off and swivelled to face him, her cheeks flushed, her mouth twisted in anger.

'What's going on with you?' She jabbed in his direction. 'We reconnected on the island.'

When he opened his mouth to respond, she jumped in. 'And I'm not just talking about the sex! You admitted you cared. It was plain to see on that documentary. So why are you freaking out? Don't you want to give us a go?'

'I did.'

Her face fell as his past tense registered.

'What changed?'

'Damn, this is difficult.'

He slid off the wall too, jammed his hands in his pockets to stop reaching for her.

'Just tell me the truth.'

Her soft sigh tugged at him, hard. She was right about one thing. He cared about her, more than she'd ever know, and he owed her some small snippet of the truth.

'When I said I wanted to talk last night, I wanted to see if you were interested in dating.'

The glimmer of hope in her eyes had him eager to finish the rest of what he had to say. 'Dating, Krissie, that's it. Nothing too heavy, too involved, just the two of us seeing each other casually.'

'Which means what?'

'Exactly that. Hanging out together, going places, having fun.'

Her eyes narrowed. 'Sleeping together.'

He nodded, hating how her less than impressed tone made it all sound so empty, so sordid.

'Just like old times.'

He knew he'd said the wrong thing the instant the words left his mouth, her chin tilting up as she glared daggers.

'Old times?'

Her voice ended on a shriek and she twirled around, stalked a few steps before turning around and marching straight back up to him, her palm slapping against his chest and shoving.

'You expect me to slip back into our old pattern, waiting for when you have a free moment to call, waiting for you to drop around any time of the night just so I can see you, waiting for whatever ounce of affection you throw my way?'

She laughed, a hollow, humourless sound that chilled him. 'I can't believe I've been so stupid. Again!'

'Krissie, it's just—'

'Save it!'

She shoved him again, dropped her hand, her head. 'Go.'

He couldn't leave like this.

'Let me take you home. We can—'

Her head snapped up, the sheen of tears slugging him. 'There is no we! Not any more.'

That was when it hit him.

After tonight, if he walked away from her, he'd never see her again.

Ironic, in putting her needs first—her need for a full commitment, her need for the perfect marriage she craved—he'd lose the only woman he'd ever loved, leaving a giant, gaping hole in his life, his heart.

Grabbing her hands, he tightened his grip when she tried to pull away.

'I don't know how to give you what you want.'

Something in his tone must've alerted her to the seriousness of his declaration for she stilled, her wary gaze scanning his face.

What seemed like an eternity later, apparently satisfied by his sincerity, she said, 'What do you think I want?'

His attention, his love, his ring on her finger. He could give her the first two; the last was non-negotiable.

'All of me.'

'Maybe I'd be happy with some?'

He shook his head. 'You shouldn't have to settle. You deserve more.'

'Spoken like every other guy trying to give a girl the old "it's not you, it's me" claptrap.'

Needing to convince her, needing her to hear him, really hear him, he said, 'Whatever happens between us, I can't promise I'll ever marry you.'

When her mouth drooped he released her hands, stepped away, hating the fact he'd made her look so sad.

'You want the perfect love. You said so. While I'd give anything to explore what we've restarted between us, I can't be that perfect guy for you.'

He rubbed the back of his neck. It didn't help, tension tightening his muscles to the point of migraine onset. 'There's no such thing as perfect.'

She didn't speak, her lips compressed, her eyes downcast, and when she finally raised them her wounded expression had him curling and uncurling his fingers to stop grabbing hold of her hands again and never letting go.

'Krissie, I'm sorry.'

'Not half as sorry as I am.'

He watched her walk away, clamping down on the desperate urge to run after her and take it all back.

CHAPTER FOURTEEN

Stranded *Survival Tip #14*
*Find humour in watching your last bar of soap
float away.*

Twitter.com/Stranded_Jared
Watch Stranded. *Interesting doco. Gong-
worthy. The producer rocks.*

Twitter.com/Stranded_Kristi
Private screening party for Stranded *debut
cancelled.*

KRISTI stared blankly at the stack of glossy brochures for the latest mobile-phone technology on
her desk. At the start of a PR campaign she'd
usually scour whatever promo material she could
lay her hands on, get a feel for what the client
wanted then brainstorm, allowing her imagination
free rein to create a whizz-bang public-relations
pitch she could deliver with pizzazz.

Her job was to make the client look good. Pity she couldn't do the same for herself.

Glancing down at her drab navy shift dress and sedate pumps, she grimaced. She hated navy, hated shapeless shift dresses more. But this was her 'I'm having a bad day' dress and people knew it. They steered clear, exactly as she intended.

Being here was hard enough without having to field countless inane questions about her time on Lorikeet Island; or, worse, her time spent with tennis pro Jared Malone.

She'd faced them all her first hour back: *what was it like being stuck on an island with a hottie? What did you do? How did you pass the time? Did anything happen off camera?*

Rubbing the bridge of her nose, she swung away from her desk, ignoring the stack of brochures in favour of the stunning Bondi view out of her window.

What was wrong with these people? Did she go around asking everyone how they passed the time with their other half or if anything *happened*?

Besides, they'd be able to see for themselves soon enough, considering her star-struck expression would be prime-time viewing for all and sundry this time next week.

Just one look and people would know exactly

how she'd spent her time on the island: swinging between moody and resentful to mooning around after a guy who didn't want her for anything beyond *casual*.

'Good to see you hard at it.'

At the sound of Rosanna's gravely voice, she swung her chair around, hoping her smile appeared genuine.

While her boss hadn't said anything after the preview screening, she knew curiosity must be eating away. Rosanna was never backward in coming forward and would have a host of probing questions waiting.

Kristi tapped the mobile-phone brochures. 'Just thinking about a new angle for these.'

'Don't bother.'

Rosanna swept into the room, balancing a thick Manila folder in one arm and a soy chai latte in the other.

'These are for you.'

Kristi's eyes narrowed as she eyed off the latte. Rosanna never brought her coffee, let alone her favourite; it was always the other way around.

As for the folder, more work. Goody. Might take her mind off the monstrous mistake she'd made in assuming Jared might actually feel something for her, that they might have a future.

Picking up the coffee, she sipped, sighed, savouring the delicious creaminess sliding over her tastebuds.

'Are you buttering me up for something?'

Rosanna perched on the edge of her desk, looking decidedly smug. 'Nope. It's a thank you.'

'For?'

'This.'

Ros tapped the Manila folder, her cat-got-the-cream smile widening.

'Remember that promotion I mentioned? All yours.'

'Really?'

In all the draining tension of the last twenty-four hours, she'd forgotten about the promotion. Once she'd handed the prize cheque to Meg, she'd been happy, her job done.

At any other time, she would've cartwheeled over her desk and high-fived Ros, but now, while she wanted to keep busy, the thought of extra workload merely added to the thick, leaden wool-liness in her head.

'I mentioned Channel Nine's upcoming reality show, *Survivor* with a twist? Well, there's another twist. They're syndicating around the world.'

'Great.'

This would be a job opportunity of a lifetime, doing the PR for a project this huge. If only she could summon up suitable excitement.

'It is for you. You're heading to LA.'

'What?'

'You heard me.'

Rosanna slid off the desk, rubbed her hands together. 'A show over there went gangbusters courtesy of some top-notch PR. Channel Nine want you to check it out, do something similar here.'

Rosanna snapped her fingers. 'Did I mention all expenses paid?'

'Wow…'

She wanted to step up the career ladder, take her job to the next level, now she could. So why the fizzle of disappointment that gaining this promotion wasn't all she'd built it up to be?

'Tell me that glum expression isn't because you'll miss lover boy? You don't leave for a few weeks, plenty of time for a long, meaningful goodbye.'

That was when it hit her.

Role reversal. Last time, Jared left because of his career. This time, it was her turn.

She should be glad. She'd wanted closure, now she'd have it, once and for all. So why the uncertainty twisting her insides into a painful knot?

Rosanna snorted, held up a hand. 'Don't tell me. By that faraway look on your face, you're imagining all the ways to say goodbye.'

Wiggling her fingers, she twirled and marched

to the door. 'I'm out of here. I'll email you all the details.'

'Thanks for the promotion.'

'You earned it, sweetie. Later!'

She had earned it.

Spending a week stranded on an island with Jared Malone, being filmed, allowing the world to see what a fool she'd made of herself…yeah, she'd definitely earned it.

Time to say goodbye to her past. Permanently, this time.

When she'd walked away from Jared last night, something inside her had broken.

He cared about her, was willing to have a relationship with her, but didn't want to marry her. Which ultimately meant he didn't love her enough, couldn't love her enough.

She should be grateful he was putting her needs first, had listened to her dreams for the perfect love. Instead, all she could think was, *What a damn waste.*

Now she was leaving and, while she'd had no intention of seeing him again after their D&M last night, this time she wanted complete closure.

On her terms.

She didn't want to spend the next six months in LA rehashing every word, every expression, of their last heartbreaking confrontation.

Uh-uh, this time, she wanted to go out knowing she'd slammed the door on any potential relationship between them once and for all.

Jared picked up the phone for the hundredth time that morning before slamming it back down.

He wanted to call Kristi.

He should call her.

Just to make sure she was okay.

Yet every time his finger had hovered over the numbers, he'd hung up, angry with his deliberating, furious with the constant twinge in his breastbone, compelling him to go to see her and apologise.

For what?

Not being able to love her enough?

Not being able to give her what she wanted, what she deserved?

Or for not being the type of man to take a risk on something—*someone*—with the potential to change his life?

He couldn't stop thinking about her.

He'd bounced into Activate at the crack of dawn, eager to bury his nose in work: ordering new equipment, ensuring the financial records were ready for a meeting with the bank, checking over the digital media package.

All perfectly legitimate stuff that could've been handled by the manager but, the more time he spent here, the more he realised the rec centre was more to him than a funding opportunity.

He wanted to be a part of it.

He understood these kids: where they were coming from, what they faced, what they were running from. He could make a difference, and not just with his money.

He had investments all over the world, had used his prize money wisely, but now he was here he had no intention of spending his retirement playing the occasional celebrity tournament or driving fast cars in Monte Carlo.

Sydney was his new home, was a good fit and he'd make sure every disadvantaged kid in the city knew they would always be welcomed at Activate.

Thinking of his involvement here brought him full circle back to Kristi. She'd been the one to open his eyes to his commitment to the place. She'd been the one to open his eyes to a lot of things.

Namely that he could love, despite long-term beliefs to the contrary.

So what was he going to do about it?

He'd rehashed their parting last night a hundred times in his head. Was he being noble in putting her needs first or was he running scared?

Scared of commitment, scared of the future, scared of loving someone so much you had to spend the rest of your life with them or shrivel up emotionally and die.

'Yo.'

Glad for the distraction from his circuitous thoughts, he glanced towards the door where Bluey slouched, his red hair bristling as much as his attitude.

'Hey, Bluey. Come on in.'

The sulky teenager didn't say a word, shuffled into his office and slumped into a chair.

Jared took a seat on the sofa opposite, glad he'd overseen his office personally. Kids wouldn't feel comfortable on the other side of a commanding desk and he hoped the modular lounge suite with comfy cushions might encourage them to heed his open-door policy.

He wanted to be available to anyone and everyone whenever he was in the centre, yet more proof of his commitment.

'Been reading your blog.'

'Yeah? What do you think?'

'Lame.'

Jared stifled a smile as he registered the first sign of anything but indifference in the boy's expression.

'Maybe you should watch the show next week. Might be better.'

'Whatever.'

Bluey focused on the rip in his dirty jeans, picking at the fray.

'Me and some of the guys want to shoot hoops. You have anything like that here?'

Wanting to punch the air in victory, Jared deliberately played it cool.

'Sure, any sport you're into, the rec centre can get equipment, set up courts, whatever you need.'

Keen not to lose the kid now he'd made his first overture, he stood.

'Want to check out the basketball court?

Bluey glanced nervously around, as if expecting someone to appear out of nowhere and give him a clip across the ear. Poor kid. He'd probably had that happen a time or two.

'We can grab a soda on the way, and a ball, maybe get in a few practice shots?'

Bluey's eyes lit up and Jared drew in a sharp breath at the unexpected surge of emotion making him want to hug the boy tight.

'Okay.'

As he fell into step with Bluey Jared knew sticking around Sydney was the smartest decision he'd made in ages.

Now if he could only solve the dilemma regarding Kristi as easily.

* * *

The hairs on the back of Kristi's neck stood to attention as she walked quickly down Darlinghurst Road, staring straight ahead and blocking out the shouts from touts outside strip joints, the abuse hurtling between two homeless guys fighting over a half-empty beer bottle and a road-rage incident between rival bikie gangs.

She'd lived in Sydney her entire life but rarely ventured down to Kings Cross after heeding her parents' warnings of assaults, robberies and drugs.

The occasional visit had been in a big group of friends, usually to the bar with the best bands at the end of the road, and while she shouldn't feel this uncomfortable in broad daylight, she did.

All the hollow eyes peering at her from between buildings, bodies wedged into the darkness, as if waiting for nightfall to come out.

A loud cackle from a nearby doorway made her jump and, feeling decidedly foolish—and more than a tad nervous—she picked up the pace, rounded a corner and breathed a sigh of relief as she spied Activate, a nondescript building with a new whitewash.

Sitting on several blocks, the centre must've been an old warehouse at one stage: high ceilings, sprawling buildings interconnected, large yard at the front.

Her first impression was welcoming as she hurried through the wide front gate, along a newly paved Bessemer path and up the steps to the double doors, which slid open soundlessly as she approached.

Jared must've spent a fortune on this place, she thought as she stepped inside, breathed in the pungent odour of fresh paint, polished wood and new leather.

The reception area, if one could call the informal entrance area that, consisted of several black and red leather sofas spaced around the walls facing each other, an antique trunk stacked with sporting magazines and a self-serve vending machine that looked as if it operated on a trust system, with a basket in front of it for donations.

While the place was empty, she could envisage it filled with kids lounging around, flipping through the magazines, mouthing off about who could do the biggest motor-cross jumps or do the biggest bombs into Watson's Bay.

The place beckoned, had a warmth missing in most kids' hang-outs, and if it could tempt a quarter of the teens off the streets of Kings Cross into here for even a short time Jared would be doing the area a great service.

Before she could head off in search of Jared, a small plaque tucked behind the front door caught her eye.

DEDICATION TAUGHT ME TO BELIEVE
MIRACLES CAN HAPPEN...IF YOU
WANT THEM BAD ENOUGH.

Kristi suspected Jared was referring to his dedication to tennis and, while that dedication had once
ripped them apart, she agreed with the sentiment.

Miracles could happen if you wanted them
badly enough: just not to her.

With Jared's recalcitrance and her promotion
on another continent, it would take more than a
miracle to get them back together. Like hell being
covered in a layer of thick, solid ice.

Heading down a long corridor, she followed
the sound of distant voices and a consistent
thumping that could only be a basketball.

The corridor ended, opened out onto a huge
indoor basketball court, the squeak of sneakers on
floorboards drawing her attention to the far end
where two figures shot hoops.

Her heart leapt at the sight of Jared, her predictable reaction having more to do with his
patience in showing a young kid how to shoot
hoops than his impressive physique.

Even from a distance, she could see the muscle
definition in his legs, the tone in his torso, the
strength in his arms as he lifted the ball overhead
and lobbed a perfect three-point shot.

The kid applauded before snatching the ball out of Jared's hands, dribbling towards the hoop and executing an impressive slam dunk.

They high-fived, resumed positions and Kristi leant against the door jamb, content to watch the man she loved yet couldn't have exhibit yet another wonderful side to him.

Shame about that miracle because, right at that very moment, she wanted it so badly she ached.

CHAPTER FIFTEEN

Stranded *Survival Tip #15*
*Scrapbooking may be fun, but choose the
memories you save with care. Glue lasts longer
than first love.*

Twitter.com/Stranded_Jared
*Check out Activate. Shoot hoops, cricket in
the nets, hang out, whatever, it's cool.*

Twitter.com/Stranded_Kristi
I'm leaving on a jet plane. Over and out. Definitely over, worse luck.

'You were great with that kid.'

A genuine smile lit Jared's face as he grabbed a soda, handed Kristi one. Her favourite lemon flavour. Was there nothing he didn't remember about her?

'That's what this place is here for, somewhere kids like Bluey can hang out.'

'I'm not talking about the place.'

She slugged back her soda, locking gazes with him over the can, wondering why he could stand in front of the world and accept a Grand Slam trophy but was reticent to accept praise over a good deed.

Shrugging, he lobbed his empty can into a bin. 'I got to mingle with kids on the circuit. Loads of talented youngsters.'

'A bit different from the street kids around here, I'd say.'

'Kids are kids the world over. Give them a cool place they can blow off some steam, they'll be there.'

'Is that what you did as a kid? Pick up a racket to blow off steam?'

A shadow passed over his face before he ran a hand over it, wiped it clean, his expression frighteningly grim.

'Yeah.'

He didn't want to talk, that much was obvious. She would've ignored his reticence, stepped around it in the past and on the island, but now she had nothing to lose.

She was leaving, and she'd be damned if she went out on a whimper.

'How old were you when you started playing?'

'Nine.'

'Is that late for a champion?'

'Depends. Kids start learning at all ages. Guess I was a fast learner.'

He spun away, his strides long as he headed up the corridor towards what she assumed was his office. She fell into step beside him, her four-inch stilettos not made for power walking as she had to sprint to keep up.

'Hey, slow down a sec.'

He stopped so fast she almost slammed into him. 'Look, I'm really busy so—'

'Too busy to say goodbye?'

'What?'

Frowning, his mouth dropped open before he quickly snapped it shut in a thin, unimpressed line.

'I'm leaving next week. Thanks to our island jaunt I've got a promotion based in LA.'

'Congratulations.'

'Thanks.'

She hated this stilted conversation, wished he would sweep her into his arms and plant a huge celebratory kiss on her lips as he once would've done.

But their time for kissing was long past. They were over, finished, and this time she'd have the full closure she deserved.

'Look, we were friends if nothing else. We shared a past, we shared an interesting week on the island. I just wanted to say goodbye face to face, that's it.'

She didn't have to spell it out for him, a flicker of guilt clouding his eyes.

'You want the goodbye you didn't get last time.'

'Uh-huh. Is that too much to ask?'

'No.'

His gaze locked on hers, the intensity slamming into her.

She opened her mouth to respond, totally losing her train of thought as he stepped closer, her heart jackknifing at the proximity, recognising how much she'd miss him.

He caressed her cheek, the barest brush of fingertips against skin that sent a shudder of longing through her. 'So this is it?'

She managed to draw air into her lungs to form the words 'This is it,' her trembling body making a mockery of her response.

He hesitated a second before crushing his mouth to hers, the impulsive kiss every bit as wonderful, as wild, as unrestrained as she remembered.

She hadn't planned this as part of their goodbye, hadn't thought beyond a civilised parting enabling her to move on with her life, but as he backed her up against the nearest wall, deepened the kiss to the point of no return, she knew her quiet, polite farewell plans had just gone up in smoke.

When they came up for air she took a step back, needing space to recover, needing air like a diver with an attack of the bends. 'You want the local kids to get some decent sex education too while they drop in?'

He muttered a curse. 'Lost it for a moment.'

'Guess we both did.'

Something she couldn't afford if she was to walk away from him, head held high.

Her first instinct to hold out her hand for a farewell handshake died at the confusion in his eyes, the pain mirroring her own, so she settled for a quick kiss on the cheek.

'Goodbye, Jared. I wish you all the luck in the world.'

While the logical part of her had already mentally rehearsed this goodbye, emotionally, the young woman who'd once loved him with all her heart wished he'd sweep her into his arms and never let go.

When he didn't speak, she turned and walked away, her heels rapping loudly in the silence, echoing the hollowness in her heart.

She'd done it.

Had closure.

So why did it hurt so damn much?

With tears cascading down her cheeks and rigid determination not to look back, she headed for the door, and missed seeing a world champion brought to his knees in defeat.

* * *

'I can't believe you're leaving.'

Meg scrubbed the kitchen bench with added vehemence, her pout reminiscent of the many times she'd tried to snaffle one of Kristi's Barbies and failed. 'And for six months! What sort of an aunt leaves Prue for that long?'

'An aunt cementing her career. An aunt hoping to fly her favourite niece over to Disneyland with the hefty raise she's getting.'

Kristi's dry response garnered the slightest smile from her sister.

'We can pay our own way, thanks to your generosity.' Meg's bottom lip wobbled before she clamped down on it with her overbite. 'But honestly, sis, I'm going to miss you.'

'Ditto, kid, but it isn't for ever.'

Unlike her break-up with Jared, the thought, sending a stabbing pain like a stake through her heart.

'Oh-oh.'

Meg ditched her cleaning cloth and flung open the freezer door, passing a tub of Turkish delight ice cream and a spoon.

'Here. Get some of this into you. It'll help whatever just put that look on your face.'

Before she could shovel the first spoonful into her mouth, Meg slapped her head, groaned.

'Tennis boy! How does your leaving affect things between you two?'

'It's over.'

Quickly spooning a mouthful of ice cream into her mouth to prevent talking, she waited for Meg to exhaust her indignation/advice/theories.

'Over? But the guy's in love with you! How could you break his heart like that?'

The spoon clattered to the floor as she gaped in shock.

'*Me* break *his* heart? Are you nuts?'

Shaking her head, Meg grabbed the tub out of her hands, rummaged in the top drawer for her own spoon, before digging it into the soft, creamy ice cream fast melting to goop.

'Tell me what happened.'

'Considering you're on his side, maybe I shouldn't.'

Stuffing a spoonful into her mouth, Meg brandished the spoon like a sword.

'Start at the beginning and don't leave anything out. Otherwise I'll stow away a week's worth of Prue's gym socks in your shoe bag.'

Unable to stifle a grin, Kristi folded her arms and propped against the kitchen bench.

'Fine. You saw how he looked on the doco. He's as smitten as I am. Then later, he gives me some spiel about wanting to date again but not being able to ever promise marriage, about not giving me what I deserve. Lame, huh?'

Meg tapped the spoon against her front teeth, the clatter annoying. 'Hmm…interesting.'

'What?'

Pinning Kristi with a probing stare she had honed to a fine art growing up, when she used to pester her with a thousand and one facts-of-life questions, Meg said, 'What are you afraid of?'

'Nothing.'

'Bull.'

Meg dumped the ice-cream container on the bench top and jabbed a finger her way.

'You must be afraid of something, otherwise why wouldn't you date and see where this leads?'

'Because I want to get married and—'

'Puh-lease! Aren't you a bit old to be hanging onto a pie-in-the-sky dream?'

Shaking her head, Kristi stared at her sister. 'What's gotten into you?'

Holding her hands palm up in surrender, Meg shrugged. 'I just don't want to see you throw something special away on a pipe dream.'

When Kristi opened her mouth to protest, Meg held up a hand. 'Uh-uh, let me finish. Last time you were heartbroken because he didn't love you enough. This time, he loves you yet you still don't want him. What do you want from this guy?'

'I want him to love me enough to give me the world!'

'Get real.'

Meg's cute little scoff would've made her laugh if she'd felt like laughing. As it was, she felt like strangling her relationship-guru-in-the-making sister.

'You're chasing perfect and there's no such thing as perfect.'

Meg gestured around her tiny cubbyhole kitchen, at the pile of homework books strewn across the table, the photos of her daughter in higgledy-piggledy disarray on the fridge, the stack of sporting equipment tumbling over itself near the door.

'This is what chasing perfect got me. You know that. So what are you doing? Giving up on a guy you've loved for ever because of some warped principle?'

Meg shook her head. 'Here's the thing. Not every marriage is as great as Mum and Dad's. They lucked in. Most don't. Surely I'm not telling you anything you don't already know?'

'Of course I know that,' Kristi snapped, hating how Meg sounded older and wiser while she sounded delusional for wanting something most people would class as unobtainable.

'Then what?'

Meg touched her arm, concern etched across

her pixie features, features creased beyond their years, and suddenly she knew.

'I *am* afraid…' she murmured, the realisation flooring her.

'Of loving Jared? That's normal—'

'No.'

Kristi grabbed Meg's upper arms, not wanting to put her sister in any pain but needing to voice her fear if only to test it out, to see if it was real.

'Of making the same mistake you did.'

Meg rolled her eyes. 'You're too smart to fall for a dropkick let alone get pregnant by him.'

Kristi gave her a little shake. 'Don't you see? You were doing the same thing I am, chasing the dream, trying to have the type of relationship Mum and Dad had. You weren't to know Duane would be an idiot when you got pregnant and do a runner.'

'Of course I was chasing the dream.'

Meg shrugged out of her grip, dragged a hand through her messy hair. 'That's why I want you to wake up and not let this opportunity slip through your fingers.'

'But he could leave me again…'

'Ah…the real fear.'

Meg snapped her fingers. 'Newsflash. Relationships evolve. Change. Hopefully grow. If not, either of you can leave. Why put all that on him?'

'Because last time—'

'Last time you were both young, immature. He was a superstar with a brilliant career ahead of him. He was *always* going to leave. You knew that.'

Kristi's mouth dropped for the second time in as many minutes as Meg had the grace to look sheepish. 'I didn't say anything at the time because you were heartbroken and later it didn't matter, but now?'

Meg shrugged. 'Now, you need to stop blaming him for walking away and maybe start thinking about why he did.'

'You think *I* pushed him away?'

Stunned by her sister's revelations, she sank onto the nearest chair and rubbed the back of her neck to ease the tension.

'Did you?'

Kristi closed her eyes, transported back to her relationship with Jared, every fabulous, exciting minute.

Sure, she'd always been more touchy-feely than him, but that wasn't a crime. Nor was texting him and ringing him countless times a day; just showed she cared. They'd been besotted, couldn't get enough of each other, yet Meg was right. She'd known he'd leave right from the very beginning, had allowed her sadness and naivety to ruin their last week together.

She jumped and opened her eyes as Meg placed a hand on her shoulder, squeezed.

'How could you have done it differently? To help make it last this time?'

She'd do a thousand things differently: she wouldn't be insecure and immature, she'd be realistic, knowing what she was getting into at the start, accepting him rather than hoping she could change him.

She'd admired her mum and dad's marriage so much, and their relationship had been all about respect, mutual admiration, trust...

'I didn't trust him enough...' she whispered, the knowledge hitting her out of nowhere and making her want to thump her head against the table in frustration.

'I've been an idiot.'

Meg grinned and bent down to give her a hug. 'More like a fool in love. Twice!'

Returning the hug, Kristi pulled back to study her sister's face. 'How did you get so wise?'

Meg wrinkled her nose. 'Try enough self-analysis, after a while you become a know-all on relationships.'

Seeing the shadows shifting in her eyes, Kristi studied Meg's face harder.

'Do you regret your time with Duane?'

'Considering Prue was the result? Not bloody

likely.' Meg's heartfelt sigh hid a wealth of emotions Kristi had no hope of tapping into. 'Do I regret being so narrow-sighted in wanting the dream the folks had I was blind to Duane's faults from the start? Hell, yeah.'

Kristi gnawed on her bottom lip, the truth behind Meg's wise words registering.

She'd been blind too, blind to everything but the truth.

She loved Jared.

Whatever he had to offer.

But now she was in a bind. Professionally, she couldn't give up on her dream promotion after she'd worked so long and hard for it.

Emotionally, she wanted to fling herself into Jared's arms and take whatever he could give.

Chuckling, Meg pushed her away. 'What are you going to do?'

'I have no idea.'

Despite everything that had happened, she still wanted that miracle.

Sadly, she'd given up on those a long time ago.

CHAPTER SIXTEEN

Stranded *Survival Tip #16*
When in doubt, run.

Twitter.com/Stranded_Jared
Never look back.

Twitter.com/Stranded_Kristi
And they say girls are fickle.

'ARE you and Kristi watching the premier together?'

Jared shook his head at Elliott, ignoring the jab of disappointment in his gut. 'Nope.'

'Why not? Trouble in paradise?'

Elliott's snigger faded as Jared shot him a death glare.

'She's leaving.'

Elliott's eyebrows inverted in twin comical commas. 'Ironic. Just what you did to her last time.'

His death glare didn't let up as his mate pronounced the fact he'd been pondering himself.

The irony wasn't lost on him either, though he'd been smart enough not to deliver her an ultimatum. Despite his newly awakened feelings for her, despite the urge to beg her not to go and give them a chance, he would never put her in a position to choose.

He knew how important her career was—hell, she'd spent a week on a deserted island with him for it!—and now it was taking off, he'd never hold her back.

Besides, he couldn't give her what she wanted.

She wanted a perfect love, a perfect relationship and, as he'd learned the hard way, there was no such thing.

What he still didn't understand was why she hadn't realised the truth either. She had two failed engagements to prove it, was hell-bent on following some warped idea that only the perfect man would fit her dream of matrimonial happiness, and if he didn't harbour his own doubts from watching his parents' monumental marriage stuff-up, he wouldn't put himself under that kind of pressure anyway.

What happened during their first argument, their first trial? Would she deem the marriage not perfect and bolt anyway?

Uh-uh, no way would he put that kind of pressure on himself. He'd be doomed for failure from the start.

Elliott stirred his double espresso faster. 'You've stuffed up again.'

'What do you mean again?'

Taking an infuriatingly long time to sip his coffee, Elliott finally replaced the cup on the saucer.

'Listen, mate, I didn't buy all that bull about you two just being good friends years ago and I'd be blind not to see what's going on between you now.'

Elliott steepled his fingers, pushed his glasses up with his pointed fingers. 'She's in love with you and you're just as bonkers about her.'

'Your point?'

'Do something about it.'

'She wants to get married, I don't, end of story.'

'Yeah, right, whatever.'

Amusement overrode his anger for a moment. 'You sound like Bluey.'

'The kid from the centre?'

'Yeah.'

Elliott stabbed a finger in his direction. 'See, that's what I don't get. You're prepared to invest in a bunch of kids who, let's be honest, might shove the whole thing back in your face, yet you won't take a chance on an amazing woman like Kristi?'

Elliott shook his head, resumed drinking his espresso with annoying calm. 'Seems pretty dumb to me.'

'Who asked you?' Jared muttered, stirring his

latte so fast the froth spilled over the top and splattered on the table.

Wisely, Elliott kept his mouth shut, giving him time to absorb, to mull…

The kids were different. Taking a risk on them was easy because he didn't love them as much as he loved Kristi and the thought of losing her if he went the whole way and gave her what she wanted…

His hand shook so much half the latte joined the froth on the table.

No way.

The M word?

No. Uh-uh. Couldn't contemplate it.

'Why don't you just talk to her? Try to reach a compromise? Perhaps she isn't as hooked on this marriage malarkey as you think?'

His head snapped up to glare at Elliott but he'd resumed drinking his coffee, staring at the next table as if the Parramatta Eels cheer squad were sitting there.

Could he reach a compromise?

Was it possible?

Was he giving up on the best thing to happen to him because of some entrenched fear of an institution that might never eventuate?

She was leaving in a week. Was it long enough to convince her how he really felt, despite doing his best to the contrary all this time?

'I'm off.'

Grabbing his keys and mobile off the table, he saluted Elliot. 'Wish me luck.'

'You're going to need it,' Elliott called out but he'd already gone, eager to tell the woman he loved the truth.

All of it.

Jared sprinted up the last few steps and burst through the snazzy glass door of Endorse This.

His knee had to be at the end of its rehab for the workout he'd just given it; running up three flights of stairs to avoid waiting for the lift had pushed its limits.

He'd been like this as a kid with tennis. Once he'd made up his mind, he threw himself one hundred per cent into a project. His sporting career, the rec centre, Kristi…he just hoped she'd go for his plan.

The outer office was eerily empty, as was Kristi's front and centre glass-enclosed office, so he headed towards the lone voice barking instructions in a nearby room.

Sticking his head around the door, he saw Rosanna on the phone, her hands jabbing the air as she punctuated her points with someone bearing the brunt of her ire.

Cringing at her last particularly nasty outburst, he stepped into the conference room.

'Hope I'm not interrupting.'

Barely glancing his way, she waved him in. 'You've got two minutes before I blast the next slacker.'

'I'll only bug you for a second. Is Kristi around?'

'Nope.'

From meeting her at the preview, Jared thought Rosanna was a garrulous woman who couldn't shut up for more than two seconds, so her brief response puzzled him.

'Any idea when she'll be back?'

A strange smile quirked her red-slicked lips. 'In about six months, give or take.'

His gut twisted as the implication sank in. 'You mean she's left already?'

For a moment, he thought Rosanna wouldn't answer, her lips compressed into a thin, unimpressed line. Then the phone rang and she snapped, 'The LA TV execs wanted her out there ASAP so they moved her departure date up. She's leaving tomorrow but don't you dare do anything to muck that up!'

'Thanks,' he mouthed, as she'd already answered her call, and sprinted back to the stairs.

If his knee had been tested before, it would be pushed beyond limits now as he flew down the stairs, skipping every second one.

Not muck up her departure plans?

He intended to do that and more.

Kristi lovingly wrapped her absolute favourite Christian Louboutin's in a shoe bag and made space for them in her suitcase. Her monstrous suitcase. That only housed shoes.

Luckily she had a matching pair of cases, though she doubted the airline would be terribly impressed with her destined over-the-limit baggage allowance.

C'est la vie—a girl trying to make an impression in LA needed her shoes.

Satisfied she'd packed enough pairs, she flipped the lid, zipped the case shut, wheeled it towards the door and plonked it next to the other.

The two stood guard, like sentinels to her new life; a life that didn't include the only man she'd ever truly loved.

While she'd pondered the revelations gained from her chat with Meg, she'd done nothing about it. She could've confronted Jared but realistically what would be the point?

Could she enter a relationship without marriage being the end game?

She'd contemplated it for an entire night, not sleeping a wink, a million questions and scenarios playing out in her head. Yet when the sun peeped over the horizon, she came to the same conclusion.

She'd be setting herself up for further heart-break, the ultimate fall, if she opened up to a full-on relationship with Jared knowing it couldn't lead anywhere.

During the long sleepless night, she'd thought about a lot of things. Her two cancelled weddings, the possibility she'd done the same to Barton and Avery as she had to Jared.

The admission didn't sit well with her, the thought she might have inadvertently sabotaged those relationships too.

Avery and Barton had been good guys: safe, steady, with dependable jobs, nice, the least likely to leave her. Exact opposites of Jared in every way. Looking back, she'd probably chosen them for that reason.

When Jared had dumped her and reports of his women started filtering through the magazines, she'd believed herself to be another conquest; he'd made her doubt her own judgement, had driven her to seek out men the opposite.

She'd stipulated long engagements both times, had gone out of her way to be demanding and fussy with the wedding plans. Both guys had been patient, which had only served to rile her further, a thousand and one small things piling up, niggling her, annoying her, until she'd finally called it off.

Yeah, she'd definitely sabotaged those relationships and the truth hurt. A lot.

She'd hurt those decent guys and all because she'd been too immature, too selfish to recognise that Jared hadn't been the only one at fault in their initial relationship; she'd done her fair share.

The thought of weddings drew her gaze to the scrapbook, sitting on the bottom shelf of her bookcase. Sadness filtered through her, wrapped around her heart, settled there like a dead weight as she contemplated what lay between its much-loved pages.

If Avery and Barton had been stand-in grooms after she'd fallen for Jared first time around, what guy had a chance of coming close to that role this time?

She loved him wholeheartedly, unreservedly.

He was The One.

The One her mum had talked about, had demonstrated with her love for her father every day of their lives.

She wanted that. She deserved that. Now, courtesy of one stubborn, commitment-phobe, she'd never have it. For if there was one thing she'd learned out of this fiasco, it was never to settle. Meaning she'd end up a scary spinster living in a tiny apartment with about a hundred cats.

Okay, so that cliché would never come to

fruition, as she was allergic to the furry cuties, but she could see it happening: her, old, alone, flipping through the scrapbook and wishing for what might have been.

Turning her back on the scrapbook, she headed for the kitchen before a loud pounding on her door stopped her dead in her tracks.

She'd farewelled Meg, had finished up at the office, so who was trying to break her door down with their incessant pounding?

'Open up, Krissie, I know you're in there.'

Her nerve endings snapped to attention at the familiar voice, her heart clenching in recognition.

She'd said goodbye, didn't want to talk to him, for they had nothing left to say.

As the pounding resumed she knew she had to open the door. If she didn't, and sent him away, she'd for ever wonder why he'd come.

Assuming her best indifferent face, she opened the door.

'You're leaving,' he blurted, his frantic gaze falling on her suitcases, his handsome face haggard.

'Yeah, you already know that.'

'But you brought your departure date forward. I almost missed you!'

She'd never seen him anything other than gorgeous and the fact he looked so awful went a small way to soothing her aching heart.

So he cared about her? Big deal. She wanted beyond caring, would never settle for anything else ever again.

'Can I come in?'

Shrugging, she opened the door wider. He stalked into the room, hands thrust in pockets, shoulders slumped, as if he had the weight of the world on them.

Quashing a surge of pity he didn't deserve, she crossed her arms, propped on the back of the sofa.

'What do you want?'

His gaze met hers, feverish, determined.

'I want you.'

Her heart gave a delighted wiggle before she gave it the proverbial whack. She already knew he wanted her; he'd proved that—and how!—the last night on the island. Problem was he didn't want her enough.

'Doesn't change anything—'

'I'm in love with you!'

Every muscle in her body stilled, along with her heart, as the words she'd been longing to hear filtered over her, processed in her brain, yet came up with a 'this does not compute' message.

How could he love her when he'd spent weeks trying to convince her otherwise?

Curious, she eyeballed him. 'Why now? You've had weeks to tell me how you *really* feel?'

Dragging a hand through his hair, he started pacing. 'I don't blame you for being sarcastic. I've been an idiot.'

'You got that right.'

He didn't halt, his long strides sweeping up and down her apartment.

'Stop that, you're giving me a headache.'

He stopped so suddenly in front of her she didn't have time to react when he swept her into his arms and squeezed the life out of her.

Burying his face in the crook of her shoulder, he murmured, 'I love you. And I'm sorry for putting you through all that crap while I realised it.'

Every cell in her body screamed to give in, to wrap her arms around him and never let go. But words were cheap; and she'd heard them all from this guy and more.

Allowing herself the luxury of momentarily melting into his embrace, she blinked back tears, steadied her resolve, before gently pushing away.

'Apology accepted.'

His eyes lit up, until she added, 'But it doesn't change a thing.'

Slipping out of his personal space, she strode to the door, gave a suitcase a little kick.

'I'm still leaving and your declaration doesn't change that.'

'I see.'

His devastated expression ripped a new hole in her heart, the bleakness in his eyes stabbing another.

'Do you? Really?'

She leaned against the door, mustered every ounce of strength she possessed. She'd need it, to walk away from him once and for all.

'I love you, I've always loved you. And you still walked away from me.'

Taking a deep breath, she deliberately calmed, banishing the hysterical edge to her voice.

'This time, I'm walking away and not looking back.'

Incredulity creased his face. 'So this is payback?'

He would think that. Had nothing she said registered?

'This is me taking control. This is me following my dream, my career. Surely you of all people can understand that?'

She scored a direct hit with her last comment as he nodded, defeated.

He swiftly crossed to the door and, seeing his intent to sweep her into his arms again, she held up both hands to ward him off.

'Goodbye, Jared.'

He hesitated, before swooping in for a blistering kiss that left her tingling all the way down to her toes.

'I'm not going to give up on us,' he murmured,

tipping her chin up, maintaining eye contact until she squirmed to escape the burning intensity.

She didn't say, 'You already did.'

Desperate to put some space between them, she headed for the kitchen. 'I need tea.'

Metaphoric speak for 'I need time to think, to assimilate, to process the fact you love me.'

'Want a cuppa?'

'Great.'

By his relieved grin, he expected her to thaw. Not likely. He loved her, she loved him. But she couldn't stop the insidious thought this was his way of issuing an unspoken ultimatum: him or her career.

Maybe it was some warped kind of payback? A thought she discounted in a second. She knew what type of guy he was, and playing games off court wasn't his forte. Whatever his reasoning for blurting his feelings now, she desperately needed time to think, desperately needed a soothing cuppa.

The way she was feeling, hopefully the tea leaves would make more sense of her swirling thoughts than she could.

The moment Jared had stepped into Kristi's immaculate apartment and seen those suitcases, his heart sank.

He'd prepared a speech about long-distance relationships and giving them a try, had wanted to convince her of his feelings, yet when he'd spied those cases all his plans had exploded in a bungled blurted admission he loved her.

He didn't blame her for being cynical. Considering what he'd been saying the last few weeks, he wouldn't believe him either.

Thankfully, she'd needed time out, had fled to the kitchen, giving him valuable space to regroup, marshal his thoughts and hope to God he convinced her to take a chance on them when she returned.

He wandered around her small lounge room, checking out photos, loads and loads of the things depicting a happy family and more recent pics of her and Meg.

In every photo, her parents had their arms wrapped around each other, her dad resting his head on her mum's, their strong bond evident. Kristi and Meg were beaming in every picture. They'd had the perfect upbringing, with parents who loved each other and obviously adored their girls.

Little wonder Kristi had some pie-in-the-sky idea about love and what it entailed.

Turning his back on the photos, he perused her bookshelf, housing everything from thrillers to historical romance.

He loved books, had hid out at the local bookshop as a kid—another escape from his parents— happily spending hours in there, skimming titles, reading blurbs but preferring cartoon magazines, eager to get lost in a world of make believe that was so much better than reality.

Tugging on the latest legal thriller to scan the blurb, he dislodged a stack of books from the top shelf, several tumbling out, knocking more off lower shelves in their journey before landing at his feet.

Squatting, he picked them up, his gaze landing on a giant scrapbook that must've fallen off the bottom shelf.

He wouldn't have noticed it if not for the picture of a young Kristi stuck on the front cover, next to the words 'MY WEDDING'.

Suppressing a shudder, he quickly glanced over his shoulder before flipping it open.

Then wishing he hadn't.

Page after page of white gowns and floral bouquets and towering cakes.

Scraps of lace and satin, old wedding invitations, saved cake bags.

Bad enough in their own right, until he came upon the last few pages…

'My Dream Wedding.'

He shouldn't have looked, should've snapped the scrapbook shut and shoved it back into the bookcase but, drawn by curiosity, he flipped the page.

And his heart stopped.

There, amidst the pictures of a simple white

floor-length gown, a two-carat princess-cut bezel diamond ring and a two-tiered white with black piping cake resembling a fancy hat, was a photo.

Of him.

'You want cookies with your tea?'

He jumped at her voice drifting from the kitchen, bundled the scrapbook and the remainder of the books back into the bookcase and stood quickly.

'No, thanks, I'm good.'

But he wasn't. Seeing him in the role of her groom had shattered every preconceived notion he'd ever had.

She thought he was her perfect groom.

He couldn't be further from it if he tried.

His first instinct was to run. Run as fast and as far as he could.

Then his gaze resettled on the scrapbook and he closed his eyes, seeing every page in crystal-clear clarity as he mentally flipped the pages.

Those pages filled with wedding memorabilia must've taken a long time, must've taken patience and care from a woman who valued an institution as old as time.

As for her chosen dress and cake and ring, someone as special as Kristi deserved those beautiful things, deserved to have the fairy tale come true.

In that second, his eyes snapped open. What the hell was he doing? He'd come here to prove his love, to convince her to try a long-distance relationship, to let her know he'd finally opened his heart enough to consider the possibility of marriage, despite the fact it scared him silly.

So why on earth would he take one look at her wedding scrapbook, a book filled with hopes and dreams and love, and want to turn his back on that?

He was an idiot.

How could he convince her to believe he'd changed his mind when he could hardly compute the change himself?

Unable to tear his eyes from the scrapbook, he stared at it…as if it were trying to send him some kind of obtuse message…and as he heard her footfall it came to him in a flash of pure, inspired brilliance.

He swiped up his keys, glancing at the kitchen in time to see her sashay out with matching teacups on a tray. Her confused gaze landed on his keys before slowly lifting to meet his.

'What's going on?'

'Don't move. I'll be back ASAP.'

'Are you nuts?'

She dumped the tea on a nearby table, disbelief warring with outrage across her expressive face. 'You barge in here, blurt you love me, now you do a runner? What the—?'

'I love you. Trust me.'

He planted a quick peck on her cheek, her spicy fragrance tempting him to linger, to haul her into his arms and never let go. There was time enough for that.

He was a man on a mission.

'Trust you?'

Her raised eyebrow said it all.

'I'll tell you everything as soon as I get back.'

She didn't move, didn't blink, the shimmer of hope in her wide blue eyes enough incentive to send him bolting out of the door.

They'd been through so much, too much. Words weren't enough any more.

She needed proof of his love.

He'd give it to her; show her exactly how much he loved her.

CHAPTER SEVENTEEN

Stranded *Survival Tip #17*
*When in need of serious forgiveness, forget the
flowers. Only one thing works. Get down on
your knees and start grovelling.*

Twitter.com/Stranded_Jared
*Whoever said actions speak louder than
words was a bloody genius.*

Twitter.com/Stranded_Kristi
*Made a list, checked it twice; typical of a guy
to throw it all into disarray.*

KRISTI paced the apartment for hours, wearing
tread marks in her favourite funky rug.

Jared was a certifiable lunatic.

Professing his love one minute, bolting out of
here the next. She should lock the door, refuse to
answer it and finish up her packing.

Instead, his sincerity when he'd asked her to

trust him kept flashing through her mind. And there was that one little salient point of him saying he loved her…

She pinched herself on the arm, again, just to make sure she hadn't collapsed onto her bed in exhaustion from packing and fallen asleep.

Ouch! Nope, still hurt, which meant she was very much awake and the guy she loved had just told her he loved her right back!

What was he up to?

The selfish part of her—which had botched her previous relationships—wished he could come with her to LA. But she'd never make that demand. She was foolish enough to push him away once, no way would she do it again.

So where did that leave them?

Long-distance relationship? Her losing concentration on the job and getting fired anyway? Exorbitant phone bills? Her life laid out on Twitter again?

None of those options appealed, which brought her back full circle to *what was he up to?*

A loud pounding had her running to the door and flinging it open, totally blowing her intention to play things cool and wait to see what he had in mind.

Before she could speak he picked her up and spun her around, the air whooshing out of her lungs, her whoop of surprise making him laugh.

'Hey! Let go…' she trailed off, her heart ka-thumping at Jared's triumphant grin.

'Sorry for rushing out like that. Important business to attend to.'

'Business? After what you said earlier?'

She shook her head, pushed against his chest until he set her down on her feet. 'You've got five seconds to explain yourself, mister, or I'm—'

'I came to give you these. Some light reading to pass the time on the long-haul flight.'

He ducked down, picked up a pile of magazines hidden behind one of the pot plants framing her doorway, and handed them to her.

Her eyebrows shot heavenward as she flipped through the stack of bridal magazines, all glossy and new and tempting. What she couldn't understand was why.

'And this, to help you hurry back.'

If the magazines confused her it had nothing on the small distinctive blue box from Tiffany resting on the palm of his hand, outstretched towards her.

Taking the magazines and dumping them on top of her cases, he pressed the box into her palm.

'Go ahead. Open it.'

No way.

It couldn't be.

Her fumbling fingers fiddled with the lid and

when she finally prised it open she exhaled on a loud woo, not computing what she was seeing.

'It's my ring.'

'I know. Not exactly the same but the closest I could get on short notice.'

He grinned, proud as a kid who'd aced his first test. 'I saw it in your scrapbook.'

If the ring had floored her, the sight of Jared Malone dropping to one knee and taking hold of her hand in her doorway almost made her keel over.

'Because I love you. Because I want to spend the rest of my life with you. Because I want to marry you.'

A faint buzzing filled her head, grew louder, as she blinked away the spots dancing a jig before her eyes.

She'd never fainted in her life but as the world suddenly tilted it looked as if there was a first time for everything.

'Whoa!'

He leaped to his feet, caught her before she slumped to the floor, her head spinning from his proposal more than a lack of oxygen to the brain.

'Not quite the reaction I expected.'

'Not quite the farewell I expected,' she countered, allowing him to lower her onto a nearby sofa where she hung her head between her knees,

took great gasps of air, finally feeling strong enough to sit up and face him.

Taking hold of her hand, he sat beside her, his body wedged tight against hers, as if he had no intention of letting her go anywhere.

'I know you think I'm a lunatic, vacillating all over the place, pushing you away one minute, professing my undying love the next. That's where this comes in.'

He toyed with the ring box in his free hand, flipped the lid open and shut, the princess diamond catching the light and sending shards of exquisite brilliance dancing around the room.

'I wanted to show you how I felt. I thought you wouldn't listen to me after the way I've acted. I'm hoping you'll believe me now.'

She didn't know what to believe.

Her dream groom had just proposed, exactly like in her fantasy. Only problem was, it had happened so fast, she doubted any of this was real.

Rubbish! You're doubting yourself as usual, trying to find a reason to sabotage the relationship for fear of making a mistake like Meg, for fear of the relationship not living up to your high expectations, for fear he'll leave you. Again.

Squeezing her hand, he said, 'Say something.'

She blurted the first thing that popped into her head. 'I'm scared.'

He slid his arm around her, hugged her tight. 'Of what? Me walking away again? Because it won't happen. Taking this step has been huge for me, I'm not about to be a runaway groom now.'

She shook her head, desperate to snuggle into him but needing to tell him the truth if they were to have any chance.

'I'm scared of having a real relationship with you.'

He frowned, confusion clouding his eyes. 'I thought that's what you wanted?'

'I do, but…'

The memory of their last phone call eight years earlier echoed through her head, the anguish, the bitterness, the resentment, closely followed by memories of Avery's stunned expression when she'd handed back the ring, Barton's sheer outrage, which had morphed into tears when she'd broken the engagement before he'd had a chance to serve a three-course dinner he'd prepared.

She'd botched those relationships. Her, with her ridiculously high expectations and utter selfishness, not the guys as she would've liked to believe, so what was to stop history repeating?

'But?'

With her mind a whir of confusion, her heart wanted to jump back into the fray. She had to tell him, there was no other way.

Laying her palms against his chest, she pushed lightly, stared up at him with hope.

'I'm terrified of mucking up again, of making you leave.'

His brow creased in confusion. 'I don't get it.'

Inhaling, she let it all out in a rush. 'I blamed you for dumping me last time. Selfish, arrogant, tennis jock choosing his precious bloody career over me when I knew you'd leave, right from the start, I just didn't want to believe it. You never made any promises, you were the dream date for six months, and I became a clinging, pathetic limpet demanding more than you were able to give.'

He opened his mouth to respond and she placed her hand over it, quieting him.

'There's more. I resented you for years, and, whether inadvertently or deliberately, I chose to date guys the exact opposite of you.'

She dropped her hand, winced. 'That didn't help either, because my old attempts to sabotage reared again and I stuffed those relationships too.'

Smart man, he didn't say a word, let her exhaust her cathartic confession.

'So here we are again. I love you, have probably always loved you, you propose and I'm not doing cartwheels. Want to know why?'

He nodded, his tender smile encouraging her to continue.

'Because there's no such thing as perfect. What if I've built up this ridiculous marriage scenario in my head we have no hope of living up to? What if I disappoint you? Or push you away? Or do a million other stupid things that'll give you no option but to leave? What if I—?'

He silenced her with a kiss, a hot, searing kiss that blazed a path directly to her heart, scorching any further protestations along the way.

Capturing her face between his hands, he sat back, stared unflinchingly into her eyes.

'What if we go into this with our eyes wide open? What if we have no expectations other than to love and trust and respect each other? What if we do everything in our power to make each other happy?'

Hope surged through her, making her body tremble.

'I kinda like your what ifs a lot more than mine.'

Rubbing noses with her, he murmured, 'Me too.'

Smiling, she tilted her head slightly, brushed a soft kiss against his lips before pulling away to stare into the handsome face she loved.

'As much as I'd love to get swept away in all this, I'm dying to know. Why the sudden turnaround?'

He grimaced, pinched the bridge of his nose, doing little to ease the sudden frown. 'Thought you might ask that.'

'Well? You going to elaborate any time soon or do I have to torture it out of you?'

He smiled at her levity, but it was a forced smile with a twist of pain.

'Your parents had the perfect marriage. Mine didn't.'

He stood, thrust his hands into his pockets, his pacing a fair imitation of what she'd done earlier. By the time they'd finished, the rug would be for the tip.

'You never mentioned them?'

'Because I preferred to ignore them.'

He stopped, his expression halfway between disgust and embarrassment. 'They were filthy rich. Self-absorbed, bored, hated each other. I was probably a mistake, a mistake that made them pay every day they had to look at me so they chose to ignore me, pretend I never existed.'

Sympathy twisted her belly at his obvious pain.

'When they weren't screaming at each other they were keeping up pretences for their equally narcissistic friends. Empty marriages among the lot of them.'

Which explained his anti-commitment stance. But there was more, she could tell by the rigidity in his shoulders, the clenched fists.

'Best thing they ever did was dump me at their exclusive tennis club. I started taking my frustrations out on a ball, the rest is history…'

'Did your success change their attitude?'

'Oh, yeah, suddenly they couldn't get enough of me. Fawning over me, turning up at all my matches—it made me sick.'

His flat tone chilled her as much as his bleak expression. 'But you know what made me sicker? The fact I cared. Whenever they turned up at a game, I was like a little kid pretending his nightmare childhood never existed, a kid craving his parents' approval.'

'There's nothing wrong with that. They're your parents—'

'Who've barely spoken to me since I blew my knee. Nice, huh?'

He resumed pacing, his expression thunderous. 'They're such screw-ups I didn't trust myself not to be like them. But you know something? I'm nothing like them! I love you and it took the fact of almost losing you to make me realise how damn much. Marriage isn't the problem. It's the people who enter into it.'

He stopped, grabbed her hands, hauled her off the sofa and into his arms.

'We can make this work. Sure, it's not going to be easy, and far from *perfect*, but it's you and me, kid, and that's already advantage Malone.'

His sincerity took her breath away, her heart expanding with so much love she could barely breathe.

'I didn't want to let emotion into my life, didn't want to take a risk on a lifetime commitment.'

He paused, searched her eyes for reassurance. 'Until now.'

Joy clogged her throat and she swallowed, saddened by what he'd been through, when she'd had the fabled perfect life he didn't believe in. For him to tell her this, unburden his soul…she now understood what drove him and all her reservations flew into the sky alongside the latest A380 she'd still have to board tomorrow.

Jared loved her.

She loved him.

What was she waiting for?

'I accept.'

Confusion clouded his eyes for a moment before realisation struck and he let out a wild whoop, kissed her thoroughly, before opening the small blue box and sliding the ring onto the third finger of her left hand.

'There. You can't get away from me now.'

She winced. 'Actually, I can. I need to be on that flight first thing tomorrow morning.'

Crushing her to him, he murmured in her ear, 'Give me a week to get the centre organised and I'll be on the first plane out. Deal?'

'You'd do that for me?'

'You know the centre means a lot to me, but I'm

basically the financier. I can do most of the work online, can always fly back when needed.'

Smiling, he cupped her cheek, the love blazing from his hazel eyes toasting her. 'It's you I can't do without.'

'In that case, you've got yourself a deal.'

They sealed it with a kiss. A long, slow, passionate kiss that elicited a long wolf whistle and hoots from her nosy neighbours who were passing by her open door.

Neither cared. They'd already had part of their lives plastered on TV.

What was another public display of affection?

EPILOGUE

Stranded *Survival Tip #18*
An island stay is temporary. A ring is for ever

Twitter.com/Stranded_Jared
Here comes the bride. She's stunning. And she's all mine.

Twitter.com/Stranded_Kristi
Who needs a scrapbook when you've got the real thing? Cue the bridal waltz. Lucky me!

Excerpt from the society pages of the Sydney Morning Star.

Fans of sport and television flocked to the harbour-side wedding of tennis champion Jared Malone and his stunning bride, PR whiz Kristi Wilde.
    The couple's relationship blossomed under our very eyes in the documentary Stranded,

viewers' interest enhanced by regular blog and Twitter updates from the love-struck pair.

The entire country waited with bated breath when our very own golden couple fled to the States for six months but in the Aussie tradition they returned for an Australia Day wedding, the hoopla surrounding the private event rivalling the latest A-list celebrity nuptials.

The happy couple released a single photo through their best man and our source, award-winning producer Elliott J. Barnaby. The beautiful bride wore a stunning Vera Wang ivory satin strapless gown with mermaid fishtail while the dashing groom wore an Armani tuxedo.

The bride's sister and sole bridesmaid, devoted single mother Meg Wilde, walked alongside her daughter, Prue, in the bridal procession. Prue, a gorgeous ring bearer, won the crowd over with her impromptu rendition of 'Chapel of Love'.

After the select few guests, including several teens from the Activate recreational centre Mr Malone supports, feasted on roasted half-duckling with seasonal greens, milk-fed veal with Gruyère and a dessert platter featuring warm quince tart, saffron and coconut crème brûlée and dark chocolate semi-freddo, they danced well into the night.

The happy couple are honeymooning at an undisclosed destination.

Stay tuned.

Or better yet, follow the golden couple on Twitter.

Twitter.com/Stranded_Jared
I always thought winning Grand Slams was the pinnacle of success. Marrying the love of my life proved me wrong.

Twitter.com/Stranded_Kristi
Dream wedding, dream man. Perfect love exists. Never give up. Winning is sublime, on and off the court!